Dear America

My Heart Is on the Ground

The Diary of Nannie Little Rose, a Sioux Girl

BY ANN RINALDI

Scholastic Inc. New York

W

Carlisle Indian School,
Carlisle, Pennsylvania, 1879

Wani-cokan-wi, Snow-Exists-Midst Moon, 1879
December 1

My teacher, Missus Camp Bell, say I must write in this book each day. She calls it a die-eerie. It is the white man's talking leaves. But they talk not yet. My words will make them talk. At first I do not know why I must do this and not the other children around me. Teacher tells it that I know some English, that she is much proud of me, but wants be more proud. And if I do this thing I can learn better the English words and soon be A-Friend-To-Go-Between-Us, like Red Road.

This would be great honor. A-Friend-To-Go-Between-Us tells the words that the whites say to the different Indian children here, and tells the words of the Indian children back to the whites. I can do some of this now. With children who are Chippewa, like Susie King, or Dora Morning, who is Cheyenne, I do the sign language we Plains people know. Then I tell the teachers what they say. No more write now. Sleep is in my eyes.

December 2

I am frightened much to do this thing. I am about a hundred miles lost at the start. But I will keep in my path and not let it run away from me. Worst bad part is Missus Camp Bell see I am frightened. With my people this is not good. We must be brave. And I was sent here to do a brave act for my people. I want to make like much smart for my teacher.

What is this die-eerie? I ask her when she first give it to me. She say it is a way of self telling. Write who you are, she say, and how you came to be. With my people, the self telling is in the naming of babies, the painting on our tipis, our weaving and bead and quillwork, our dancing. To say his own worth, a warrior tells of his deeds in battle or on the hunt.

I have been on no battles or hunts. Of what worth am I, a girl of twelve winters? They take the lights now. I must go to my pallet and sleep.

December 3

Very cold. The *hanwi*, night sun, is *yaspapi*, bitten off. White people say it is the old moon. Two other girls who sleep in my room go under the blankets. I have a candle.

I have think of my worth. I am the eyes of my *tunkan*, grandfather, Black Cloud. His eyes are closed now. He tell me, go to white man's school so I can learn their ways. He tell me our ways are done. In The-Time-That-Was-Before, our chiefs have made large mistake in giving over our lands. The whites swarm on them like locusts. They cut the trees, spoil the hunting, make us live on reservations, and pay us ann-u-itee for the land the chiefs sold. Then they make us owe them money. Nine dollars for small bit of sugar, eighteen for bad pork, ten for sour lard, and more for bad meat, when in The-Time-That-Was-Before we got all these things from our mother the earth. And no ann-u-itee money is left. And we starve. Grandfather tells it that there is nothing on the reservation for the young people. His eyes are closed, but I think maybe so, he sees things others do not see.

My *atku*, father, is White Thunder, chief. If I came of age to wed before our ways were done, the man, he puts on his best robe and walk by our tipi. Then he come closer and grab of me. I would struggle, but he would win. If I like him

I bring him water and ask him to come another time. When he come back I make food and give him of it to eat. If I wish to be his wife, I make him moccasins, with quill-work. Then we stand in front of my father's tipi and he wraps his robe around me so all to see.

Days are going by and the nearest kin of this man visit my father and talk of the worth to be paid for me. In The-Time-That-Was-Before my father be given at least five horses. And buffalo skins. My father would look with favor on this and give a tipi, two robes, a bone awl and sinew thread, a cooking pot, ax and knife. I be given a dress of soft deerskin. This is my worth if our ways were not done. I am Lakota Sioux girl, daughter of White Thunder and Goodbird.

I am think I am cheated. For why? Because I am too young to know The-Time-That-Was-Before. I am think, also, that my new name should be Learns to Write. I have start this self telling.

December 6

I have not time to self tell for two days. They keep us busy. Rise at thirty after five when bells ring. This is sound

6

to break on the ears. First meal of day at ten and five after six. All day school and work. Evening study. Word study. Meetings to pray. One thing I learn since I have come here in *Waniyetu-wi*, Snow-Exists-Time Moon, which the white people call No Vember. The white people cut time into little pieces each day. They have round things that tick and they call clocks to show the cut-up pieces. I cannot yet understand all the cut-up pieces. They are always looking at these clocks and running.

With my people we have *anpao*, before sunrise, *anpa*, sun-shines, *htayetu*, fading-time. We have *hancokaya*, night-middle-made. We have also winter counts that tell the years by what happened.

I was born in year A-Shoshoni-Who-Entered-Our-Camp-Was-Killed. I was born in year 1867.

December 7

Another thing I have learn. The white people are very powerful. They know almost everything on the earth's surface and in the heavens, also. So much to learn! Like, what is this Vember that they want none of in Snow-Exists-Time Moon? It must be snow. Missus Camp Bell tells it that home on the reservation in No Vember they had much snow and cold. And here we still had sun and sweet grasses. At home there will be much visits back and forth in the tipis. Much talk and storytelling. Men will sit long after night-middle-made and smoke. At home now I would spend hours at the plum-pit game.

December 8

I have not see my brother Conrad Whiteshield in seven suns. Girls and boys keep their blankets in different houses here. He is my *tiblo*, my older brother, so I am to honor him. But how can I do so? He is fifteen winters and large spoiled. He much time acts like a fool. I worry for him. He does not wish to be here. On the way here he made much trouble on the boat.

At home he went on a vision quest to find his spirit helper. But he failed. He was to try again when it was told to him he must go to the white people's school. To make it worse bad, my father ask of me and not my brother to do a brave act at the school. If my brother find out this, he will no more say words to me.

When I see him last time here at school, he speak to

me. I get much happy. But I soon find his words are not good. "They say I must learn to use the word *ferment*," he tells it. "So I write: I will not ferment in the house. Other boys laugh. Teacher not laugh."

Of this he is much proud. Whiteshield is always trouble.

December 9

My feet hurt. They not yet feel at home in shoes. I want for my beaded moccasins, but they are taken from me.

December 10

Missus Camp Bell asks one sun ago to see this book. When I show her, she reads my writing and I am getting much excited to know I have write something a white person can read. She makes smile and tells it that my writing hand is good. But you must improve your grammar, she say. I ask what is this grammar. She again smile and say you will soon know. Then she say I should have write that I long for my moccasins, not that I want for my moccasins. I am confused. Is not long the opposite of short? I ask. She say yes.

But my moccasins are short, I say. I do not have big feet. How can I long for my moccasins? She smile once again and say I should keep writing and I will soon learn how some white man's words have two meanings.

I know this to be true. All my people do. In their treaties, the whites make two meanings for their words. That is how they take our land. But I do not tell this to Missus Camp Bell.

December 11

Snow today. But not much. All the white teachers get much excited and run about. The snow makes me think of home. I miss the blanket of my kin. I miss my friend Pretty Eagle. Many time in the snow we go together with Grandmother's dogs to get wood, and have fine time on the way. But we are much warm here in our class rooms and dor-mi-tor-ees where we sleep. For the first time I am almost glad for the citizens' clothes they make us wear, though my feet still hurt. I think I should maybe write about home and how I come to be here. The day she read this book Missus Camp Bell say I should.

"Do not be fear full," she say. "Face what frightens you."

I think Pretty Eagle would like her. I think Missus Camp Bell would make a good Sioux woman, but for the pieces of glass she wears on her eyes to better see.

So I write of how we come to be here. But not now. Red Road has come in. I have not see her in many suns. She is my friend from home, and came much close to be more. My father wish one time for her to be second wife. She is much pretty and good and teach me to weave baskets and do beadwork.

My mother is jealous of Red Road because she is so young and pretty. She say if my father bring Red Road to our tipi, she leave. This is not worthy of a true Sioux wife, but my father has a weakness of the heart. He is too good. My mother know this. So my father does not bring Red Road to our tipi even though it would bring much honor to us. She is daughter of Spotted Tail, our chief. She is eighteen winters and now wed to Charles Tackett, who traded with us at Rosebud Agency on our reservation. From him she learns the white man's words, then teach them to me when I go to her tipi for to learn quillwork. But I must sneak off like a fox to her. My mother is much yet jealous. Red Road and Tackett come with us to this place called Carlisle to act as A-Friend-To-Go-Between-Us.

I must go now. Red Road has cake from the kitchen. We are always hungry.

December 12

Time to write now how I come to be at this place called Carlisle in the land of Penn-syl-va-ni-a. There, I have learned the spell of it. I think I have become a word hunter. Missus Camp Bell give me another book called a dic-tio-nary. She teach me how to hunt up the words. I now have a hunting ground all my own.

I come from the place called Dakota. My people belong to the Great Plains tribe. Our men are very brave and honorable. Our women are noble. At one time my people ruled much good land — all the Black Hills, which the whites give us in a treaty in the year They-Killed-One-Wearing-A-Striped-War-Bonnet, 1868. Then the white man finds gold in the Black Hills and the treaties are forgot. My people are put on reservation on the Missouri River. But Chief Spotted Tail will not live there. Chief Red Cloud say no also. They take their people to the west of this place to be free. Finally the white man makes new reservation west of the Missouri River. Rosebud for Spotted Tail. Pine Ridge for Red Cloud. This is where Mister Captain Pratt come two moons ago, in *Canwape-kasna-wi*, Tree-Leaves-Shaken-Off Moon, white man's October. He come to ask for children for his school in the land of Mister Penn.

No more time now. They take the lights. This self telling is more hard than I think. Must tell another day of time on trains and first days here.

December 13

We have many teachers here. I would like to have just Missus Camp Bell. She smells like the prairie and is much kind and today opened a big book and showed us Dakota Territory. It was my first time to see a map. She showed us mountains and rivers.

Other teachers are not so nice. We have names for them. Mister Graystone we call Gray Beard. He teach history. Miss Monk is much skinny. She teach us sew-ing. We call her Miss Chipmunk. Miss Rosecrans has very red face. She leads the sings. She is Miss Red Corn. Then there is Woman-Who-Screams-A-Lot. She is bad to the eye. Fat and ugly. She is in the kitchen where we learn to cook. Woman-Who-Screams-A-Lot is called Missus Cafrey. She tells us that our first month here was like holy day. She says holy day is over and now we are given chores. She say to me and other Sioux children, our people may have killed Custer three years past, but we don't best her.

My people did not kill Custer. Those who did were Cheyenne and other Sioux tribes. Spotted Tail kept his people at peace at that time. But Missus Cafrey would not let me tell this. She makes me and Almeda Heavy Hair, who is also Sioux, and Dora Morning, who is Cheyenne, wash pots. She makes Ada Fox Catcher, who is Apache, scrub the floor. She makes Frances Bones, who is Comanche, clean the big stove. Kitchen must be clean before we cook, she say.

All the time she holds a big knife. I think she fears us. I think if she was at Little Big Horn she would kill Chief Sitting Bull of Cheyenne nation all by her own.

No time to self tell about past now. Too tired from washing pots.

December 14

This day I see my brother, Conrad Whiteshield. I come from across the yard. In my apron were many pine cones for

Missus Camp Bell. My brother was by the fence with another boy. When I go close I see they have *kin-ni-kin-nic*, tobacco. They are smoking.

"This is Alford Two Leggings," he say in our language. "Do you recognize him?"

I say no. The boy looked angry.

"He is Pawnee," my brother tells me. "He was once a prisoner in our camp."

I remember the time we had a Pawnee prisoner. But I had never see him. Now he is friends with my brother. Is this good? I do not know. Many of us have meet children of other tribes. First they do not come forward when we say *how kola*, hello friend.

"You are all Indians," Mister Captain Pratt tells us, "and all in the same boat. You should try to be friends." Which only confuse us because we are in no boat.

This Pawnee boy. I think he is bad medicine for my brother. They seem to keep the fire of hate alive between them.

"You will be in trouble with store cigarettes," I tell my brother.

Only he smiles. On the way here, on the boat, he and other boys get cigarettes from a trader. Mister Captain Pratt buys many more from the trader and gives to all the boys to have a smoke and say good-bye to tobacco because there is rule against it at school.

"You think I care about trouble?" he asks today in our language.

He hates his teachers, he tells it. He hates his chores. He hates baths. I think he hates me. He wants to go home for the buffalo hunt. I say there are no more buffalo. He says no matter, he wants to go home. He misses his pony. He and Alford Two Leggings will run away. But first he must change his name. Conrad was bad pick. Some older boys call him Corn Bread. Others call him Corn Rat.

"Next time some chiefs come with blanket Indians, we will leave with them," he say.

I am surprised my brother would say "blanket Indians," the word given by whites to Indian children who first come here. "Of what use is a new white name if you plan to run?" I ask him.

"From this day on I am Charles Whiteshield," is all he say.

December 15

I have been much busy. No, I have been very busy. Missus Camp Bell again read my di-a-ry and said it was *very* good, and told me some better words. So I am us-ing them. Before I would say *I am use them*. Now I say I am us-ing. "Drop the *e*, when you add *ing*," she says. Where should I drop it? I ask. She laugh. I am much further on the path than the other children. When I first come here I already know *stand up*, *sit down*, *walk softly*, and *speak louder*. Many of the boys and girls have trouble learning these words. I easy learn words like *school room*, *cottage*, *dining room*. One time I help Missus Camp Bell by using cards to teach the others. But I did not know that rakes had teeth, that fingers have nails, and tables have legs. So much to learn. My path is often tangled.

December 17

These white people get much excited about something they call Christ-mas. Missus Camp Bell explain that it comes in eight suns. Missus Camp Bell put pine cones I picked from ground around dining room. Miss Red Corn make us prac-tice many songs. Other teachers have take branches from tree-that-blooms-all-winter and put them on stair rail and on shelf over fireplace. They have bring tree-that-blooms-all-winter into house and we girls made from color paper, rings that we put together. We made pop-corn on strings.

This Christ-mas is the day their Jesus god was born. When Missus Camp Bell tells this, some girls make silly. "Did you see this baby?" Lena Blackbear asks. She is Comanche. Missus Camp Bell says she read it in the Bible. "How silly not to see a new baby," Lena Blackbear teases.

In Sunday school preacher man tells us about Jesus god. And how he was born in a stable because the white people would not let his mother into the tipi. I think the white people are selfish. Then the preacher tells us when this baby was born there was a great star in the heavens. A sign. We know about signs. We have many signs that have to do with the earth and moon and stars. But I do not understand what this has to do with bring-ing pine cones into the house. So we just sit in Sunday school and let the preacher man talk to himself.

December 18

There will be much feasting for Christ-mas. In the kitchen Woman-Who-Screams-A-Lot has us stir-ring and chop-ping and mak-ing. We make biscuits, pies, ginger-cakes. There will be gifts for us. Miss Red Corn say that on Christ-mas morning we will sing like angels. "What are these angels?" I ask. Then she tell how they come when Jesus god is born. Then I understand. They are powers. They are spirits. She teach us to sing a song about night that is silent. I think it is very pretty, but not pretty like our songs. Also we will not have to study or work on this Christ-mas. Maybe then I can do more self telling about how I come to be here.

December 21

Missus Mary Hyde is the ma-tron over all the girls in the dor-mi-to-ry. In the room with me I have Frances Bones and Almeda Heavy Hair. Across the hall are Belle Rain Water, Helen Breathes Fire, and Maggie Stands Looking. All older. All trouble. Everyone knows this and stays far from them.

Belle Rain Water is large and her face has the marks from the spotted sickness. She is much ugly. No, she is very ugly. She is both. Maggie Stands Looking is daughter of American Horse who is a chief of the Red Cloud Sioux and thinks much of herself. She does not make clean her part of the room. Missus Mary scolds Maggie for this. Before all the words got past Missus Mary's lips, Maggie Stands Looking slaps her in the face. Everyone stares. Nobody speak.

Then Missus Mary speak. "Why, Maggie?" she ask.

We all think Missus Mary would slap Maggie back. But Missus Mary look like she want to cry. I know if Missus Mary slap Maggie back there will be a big fight and Maggie will win. Maggie wants a big fight to show Missus Mary how brave she is. But when no slap comes, Maggie throws her arms around Missus Mary and cries.

"Maggie, you will keep your things in order, won't you?" Missus Mary asks.

Maggie cries more, but now her part of the room is clean, always.

December 23

Missus Camp Bell ask to read my book again. When I give it, she frowns and says, "Slapping a teacher is a serious offense. Maggie Stands Looking must be punished."

"No," I beg, "please. The council fire burns bright between Maggie and Missus Mary now. If you punish Maggie, it will go out. And all will know how you find out. They will give me new name. Girl Who Gossips."

For a more long time she has no words.

"How can I self tell in my book," I ask, "if you use my words to make trouble?"

"Do you like writing in your di·a·ry, Nannie?" she asks.

"The di·a·ry is my friend. One day soon my friend Pretty Eagle will come here. The only friend I now have is Red Road and she is in another house and so busy I don't much see her. When I do this self telling, things that were all wrong come to seem all right."

"Then I will no longer read it," she tells me. "You may write what you wish. If you wish to show it to me someday, you may, but I will in·trude no more on your thoughts. But you must do very well with your grammar in class, or I will start to read it again."

What is this in-trude? I do not know, but I feel like when they first gave me a banana. What is this banana? I ask. They showed me how to peel back the skin and it is very good. It is the same with many of Missus Camp Bell's words. When I peel back the skin, I find they are good.

December 25

No school. No work. First we hear bells. Miss Red Corn is in the hall. She say the bells are from Saint Pat-rick's church in town. We all put on new dresses we made in sewing. We older girls stand on the bal-co-ny outside and sing. From inside we hear cries of small children who are finding the stockings we helped fill and put at the end of their beds. In the stockings we put orange, apple, candy, and small gift. After we sing we go back inside and down to sitting room where the tree-that-blooms-all-winter stands. Under it are gifts for us.

Missus Pratt tells it that the gifts come from Quaker women in Phil-a-del-phi-a. Our gifts are this: candy. And oranges. New warm mittens and scarfs and hats for the cold weather. Books and ribbons for our hair. Lace collars. Soap that smells strange and sharp.

The boys go to church in town. Girls and small children go here to Sunday school. After I see my brother in yard. Everyone talks and plays. We kick balls around and run races.

"Why are you smiling?" my brother ask in our language.

"Because they give us many fine presents," I say.

"When an Indian becomes like a white person, he loses his face."

"I will not lose my face." I am angry. But I see this only pleases Whiteshield. He wishes to make me angry. And filled with guilt because some things here make me very happy.

In the dining hall the tables are heavy with food, but my brother is still not smiling. Red Road comes to sit with me. She has a new shawl and cal-i-co dress and looks very pretty. She has taken a new name. Amelia. I cannot fix this name on her. To me she will always be Red Road.

We speak in our language. "I miss you," I say.

"I miss you, too. But I hear from Missus Campbell that you are doing well."

"She is kind."

"Yes." Then Red Road peers in my face. "What is wrong, Nannie? I can see something weighs on your heart."

"My brother, Whiteshield. I worry for him. He looks for trouble."

"He always did. Why should he be any different here?" Red Road asks. But it is not said in anger. I know there was a time when Whiteshield liked her as much as I. Maybe so, he still does, I think.

"If you had wed my father, he would be different," I told her. "You could have helped him."

"Perhaps I still can," she said. "I will seek him out and speak to him. I will remind him of the old ways."

But the old ways are done, I think. If they were not, we would not be here. Still, I am very grateful to Red Road. She was almost another mother to me. Now she is my sister.

In the hall I see Woman-Who-Screams-A-Lot. She smiles at me. I do not know who this Jesus god is, but if he can do all this he must be a good medicine man. Maybe so.

Still December 25, but *htayetu,* fading-time

In the hall I looked in the mirror. I still have my face. They will keep the lights on longer this night. Some girls are reading. Some are resting. Some are gathered in our dor-mi-to-ry, telling tales of home. I write.

In *ptanyetu*, changeable-time, the white man's autumn, comes Mister Captain Pratt to our reservation, with a lady called Missus Mather. He asks Spotted Tail for children to take east to the white man's school. At first ask Spotted Tail say no. He tell Mister Captain Pratt that the white people are all thieves and liars. They took all our land. And he will give no Sioux children to learn such ways.

Then Mister Captain Pratt tell Spotted Tail he is re-mark-able man. His name has gone all over Unit-ed States and even across the great waters. But that he signed papers with the government and gave the land because he not know better. He not ed-u-cat-ed. Mister Captain Pratt ask for children of Spotted Tail and Red Cloud for to make them ed-u-cat-ed. But if they not give he will get Kiowa children, Comanche and Arapahoe children. They will be book smart and Sioux children will not.

After much big talk Spotted Tail gives five children, one who is Red Road. Others are younger boys. Two Strike gives two boys, Milk gives boy and girl, and my father White Thunder give me and my brother. No more time tonight. They take the lights. I must sleep.

December 30

In the kitchen I get in trouble. Woman-Who-Screams-A-Lot wants Lena Blackbear to make butter. I have eat this butter at table but do not know how it comes to be. I wish to watch. Woman-Who-Screams-A-Lot comes over to me. "Have you nothing to do?" she asks.

"I want to see this butter come to be," I say. "We did not have butter at home. We pounded and boiled buffalo bones for the rich oils instead."

She gets angry. "Go and make your cornmeal pudding," she yells. I did not have a pot, so I borrow one from Almeda Heavy Hair. When I give pot back, I leave some pudding in the bottom. With my people, when a family borrows a kettle you must leave a small bit of food in bottom, or you cannot borrow kettle again. A Sioux woman must always know what is cook in her kettle. Woman-Who-Screams-A-Lot said my pot was not scoured clean and made me wash all the pots.

I see she has forgot all about Jesus god day. I was long in kitchen scouring pots and my hands much hurt. But my honor is hurt more.

Tehi-wi, Hardship Moon
January 1

It is day one of the white people's new year of 1880. More feasting, but no presents. White people are very much silly on day one of their new year. But I am glad for it give me time to write.

Back home I was in the tipi of Red Road when word come to us that I am one of the children to go to school in the land of the white people. I had take the way of the fox to the tipi of Red Road, sneaking. If my mother knew, she would let fly at me words like poison arrows. My mother refuse to allow Red Road near our tipi since she will not let her be second wife. So the path between my mother and me is filled with rocks.

Word that I was to go east to school was bring by Whiteshield. My brother stands, his face full of storm, as I tell Red Road I do not wish to go.

"I do not wish to leave here," I said. "I am very frightened."

"You must," she tells it. "You must learn the white people's ways. To help our people. You will see great trees with red apples. You will ride on the iron horse. You will wear a school dress."

All these things are dust to me. "I cannot leave," I say again.

"You are not happy here," she say. "You fight with your mother all the time. You must sneak to see me. This is not good. And our people are poor now. You must learn to make your way in the white world, or you will be poor also."

I tell her I do not care about poor. I do not care about my mother. I love my people, my life. I have my pony. Red Road herself was teaching me to make beautiful baskets and paint deerskin. I love the long winter days when the elders sit around telling stories about The-Time-That-Was-Before. I love my grandmother and grandfather, my father, my brother, grandmother's dogs, the plains, the wildflowers in the spring. I am a child here. I will be a woman here, I tell it. Someday I will take a warrior husband.

Red Road is kind, but her words hurt. "There are no more warriors," she say. "And your brother is going. Didn't you just hear it from his lips?"

I look at my brother. In those days we are friends. He does not tell my mother of the time I spend at Red Road's tipi. But his face is still full of storm. "You hear it from my lips but not from my heart," he says. "I was named to go but

I'm not going. How can I leave? I still have my vision quest. How can I find a spirit helper in the east?"

Red Road talks to both of us. And her words are not empty gourds, with nothing inside to quench our need, but full of meaning, from which I drink hope.

"You know I am going," she says.

"Yes," I said.

She smiles. "My husband, Charles, is going as A-Friend-To-Go-Between-Us. He does not wish me to be without him. I will be a friend to you there as I am here."

I feel hope, but as I look around our camp I know I can see every path in it with my eyes shut. Every path in the fields and plains, the same way. How could I leave this place? It is all I know. Inside me I feel a pain, as if I am gone already. Part of me is missing. I feel like a young warrior in our Sun Dance, who has had the skin near his breasts cut and sticks put in the openings. The sticks are fastened to two ropes and I am left hanging, to show my bravery.

Only when we get to the tipi of my father do I look up and see Whiteshield on his pony, riding off toward the plains. "The white people will kill us," I tell my father.

He is wearing his chief's garments. A shirt with fringe and beaded bands on the shoulders and sleeves. Also his chief's leggings with beads, his bear claw necklace, and his braids are wrapped in otter tails. On his head is a stick headdress. I know he wears it to show the white people who we are. But no other men on the reservation wear their chief's clothing. I think my father wishes to be what he once was, maybe so.

His face is sad. I know it is because Red Road is leaving. He still yearns for her. But there is a larger sadness there, too. "You must not think of your fears now," he tells me. "You know how you always wanted to go on your vision quest?"

I say yes. But girls do not do those things.

"You have a vision quest now. Do good. It will be hard, but you will find your way."

"To do what?" I ask.

To be brave, he tells it. Then he says I must study and work and obey, and do one act of bravery. Then come home and tell him about it. I must bring him honor with this act.

I asked him if he would also ask one act of bravery from my brother.

But only he shakes his head and says I am the one to bring this honor to my family. He says my brother is older, but I am wiser.

I remind him that in order to be brave I must have a

spirit helper. And I will not find any wolves, bears, foxes, or coyotes in the white people's land.

He tells it then that the spirit helper need not be ferocious or large. And that I will know mine when I see it.

I feel my skin ripping when I say good-bye to Grandfather. He is getting so old. I fear I will not see him again. "You are my eyes," he tells me. "I remember The-Time-That-Was-Before, but it is only in stories now. You will see The-Time-That-Is-To-Be, and come home and tell me about it."

Grandmother gives me small deerskin squares into which she sews tobacco and red willow bark. "These are to burn for sacrificial offerings when you have need," she says.

My grandmother, mother to my father, has powerful medicine. She has visions. She tells them to the shaman, our holy man, who explains it to our people. In The-Time-That-Was-Before, her visions tell of attacks of warring tribes, of times to go on a hunt, or who will be a new chief. In these times she picks the place for the Sun Dance. Her last vision tells us people will come and ask for children. But the chiefs do not think it will be white people. Not many women have visions. Grandmother has told it to me that she will help me do it when I get older. Now I must go from her.

My mother does not wish me to go to white people's school. When I tell her, she laughs. "What will you learn? To be more silly than you are?"

"I will learn to read their talking leaves," I tell her. "Learn the names of their many fires, which Red Road says they call their states. Understand their language. If our elders had done this, they would not have signed away the land."

My mother, Goodbird, is daughter of a chief who sign away our tribunal homelands almost thirty winters ago. I know I should not speak such words to her, but I do.

"You go because Red Road goes," she spits at me. "You turn your face from your people. Go then. Go with Red Road. See what you learn."

My mother's angry words cut at me. She refuses to understand. So I go to see my friend Pretty Eagle, who is making sick in her mother's tipi. Pretty Eagle gets the fainting sickness. She was to go with us, but because she is still weak from her last spell, she cannot go. I hold her hand.

"You will be well soon," I say. "Then you will come. Your father tells me this."

Only she smiles at first. Then she speaks. "Yes. After the

winter becomes spring I will come east. By then you will have learned much and teach me."

No one knows why Pretty Eagle lies with the fainting sickness. Her mother and father say she dies and comes back to life. Her spells come on her at any time. One time we were out on the plains, riding our ponies, when a spell comes. I hold her hand all the time. For two moons I guard her. When she opens her eyes she is more pretty and strong than before. She has great strength, too, in her spirit. "We will hunt and bring down a bear, like the boys," she says. "We will gather all the wildflowers on the plains and put them in front of every tipi. Or we will give all the stars in the sky new names, which only we will know. We will sneak water to the warriors at Sun Dance time."

We do all these things together. I think sometimes that Pretty Eagle is going to be a shaman, even though she is a girl.

I say good-bye to everyone. Then to Grandmother's dogs, who are smart and noble and carry the wood for her on the travois. I take my bone ring teethmaker I have keep since I was a baby. The little wooden turtle with its back done in colors. I start to pack my good deerskin dress with the painted designs and the flounce decorated with pony

beadwork. Then Red Road tells me: "Do not bring anything you hold dear. When you get there they will take
from you your clothes and give you others. My husband
heard this from Pratt himself."

I leave my good blanket and take my worn one. I leave
my moccasins with the quillwork. My heart is on the
ground when we leave in the wagons. I wonder what act
of bravery I can do to make everyone proud. I fear what
lays ahead of me on the path.

The wagon is very full. All the Sioux now want to send
their children. Mister Captain Pratt leave some. Must stop
now. They take the lights.

January 3

Cold and snow. In sewing class we moved to a small
room that has a better stove. They are placing pipes in
our big sewing room. Miss Chipmunk say warm will come
in the pipes. I think of the fires in our tipis at home.
I hope my people keep warm. I think of Pretty Eagle. I
think I should have given her my good blanket and
my moccasins with the quillwork. She is often cold in
winter.

January 4

I look around all ways to find a brave deed to do to make my family very proud. But there is none. I look, also, for my spirit helper. All I see are sheep in the fields, cows in the barn, cats in the yard. One cat looks fierce, like it would be a good spirit helper. But when I speak to it, all it does is wash its face.

January 5

Today Missus Camp Bell makes me write a com-po-si-tion. I must make sentences out of three words — *wagging, promptly,* and *indeed.* So I write:

"Three winters past I see many horses wagging tails in the summer because great many bees out there. They all bite horses. Some of the horses have a short tail they are wagging very hard indeed. Because they are wagging it very promptly in every way, they never stand still. The bees have sharp teeth."

Missus Camp Bell frowns so she looks like owl who has lost the mouse he would eat. "Your grammar is de-plor-a-ble," she say.

So I must go to her class after school and chores and learn about tenses. For two weeks.

January 20

For two weeks I had to study so hard I thought my eyes would close forever, like Grandfather's. Here is what I have learned.

Tenses: This is what I have written (not write). Three years ago I saw (not see) many bees. They all bit (not bite) the horses. Some of the horses had (not have) a short tail. They were wagging (not are wagging) them very hard because there are a great many bees out there. Because they were wagging their tails very promptly in every way, they never stood (not stand) still. The bees had (not have) sharp teeth.

This is because what I saw happened three winters ago, in the tense that is past. I am still confused. So I had to learn the right way to use *see-saw*, *says-said*, *come-came*, and all other words that live in the place called tenses. I have written these words over and over. I have learned not only to drop *e*'s but to added *ed*. When cornmeal was done yesterday it was cooked. When I do it now, I cook. I will not make more mistakes. But I think the white's man's language is de-plor-a-ble. I think it matters not how I came to be at this place. But that I am almost sorry to have come. There is too much to learn. I do not see Red Road that much, she has her own classes and duties as A-Friend-To-Go-Between-Us. She lives in her own house with her husband. I miss Pretty Eagle, and much as I seek it I cannot find a brave deed to do to make my family proud.

January 22

Today was de-plor-a-ble. I have looked in my hunting ground book and found what it means. Bad medicine.

Today my brother shamed us all. It was very cold and there was snow on the ground, but early this day we heard war whoops from the yard. Everyone got up from warm beds to look out. There was a strange figure carrying a torch and doing a dance.

He was wearing only a breechclout and moccasins. In his belt he had a knife. Around and around he danced while he chanted a war song.

"It is Charles Whiteshield!" said Lena Blackbear. "Your brother! Oh, he is fine. And listen!"

We watched the war dance and listened to the chanting. It echoed off the buildings and filled the night. I had tears in my eyes. It reminded me so much of home. And I could feel my brother's pain, as he sang. But where had he gotten his breechclout, moccasins, and knife? They take all our blanket Indian things. No matter. Soon the yard was filled with light, and Gray Beard came to bring Whiteshield inside. Gray Beard was much angry and would strike my brother if he could. He took Whiteshield's knife, then pulled him by the arm inside the boys' house. Now Whiteshield will be punished.

January 24

Today they let me go to the guardhouse to see my brother. "Why did you do this thing?" I asked him.

"I am a warrior," he says.

"You are only a boy of fifteen."

"I have counted coup. I am a warrior."

This is true. And not true. He has touched an enemy with his lance, like young braves must do many times to become warriors, counting each one as they do so. But he did not kill the enemy. Whiteshield touched a Crow scout with his lance one morning early. My father found the scout spying at the edge of our camp, killed him, and invited my brother to touch him with his lance. My brother was only twelve when this happened, but everyone was proud. He had struck his first coup. They gave him a great feast. And Whiteshield has never forgotten it. He became spoiled because of it.

"You are no warrior," I ~~tell~~ told him again. "A warrior does not shame his people."

He becomes angry. "I will soon be a warrior. I will soon go home and do my vision quest."

I asked him if he ever thought this school could be his vision quest. Only a stupid girl would say such a thing, he tells me.

Tears came to my eyes and I asked my brother why he hated me so.

Then he ~~sneers~~ sneered and told me he knew that Father asked me, not him, to do the act of bravery. And he is the son.

So, I thought, that is the spring from which his anger swells. And his spring is poisoned with anger. I should have known he would find this out.

Because he did a war dance in the yard with his Indian things, my brother now spends five days in the guardhouse on bread and water. I must try twice hard now to find my act of bravery. To wipe away the shame Whiteshield brings us.

January 30

We learned about the Devil in Sunday school. I think he is like some of our medicine men. He can change his shape if he wishes.

I like Sabbath day because we have more time to ourselves. Now I will write about our trip.

When we ~~leave~~ left our reservation with Mr. Captain Pratt my brother still could not be found, so we ~~go~~ went without him. We stopped at Pine Ridge, reservation of Red Cloud. There we took many more children. Red Cloud gave a grandson. American Horse gave two sons and his daughter, Maggie Stands Looking. From there we travel-ed to the steamboat landing. My brother was there waiting on his pony. He and a friend rode fifty miles to meet us after my father found him. I do not know what father said to make him come. But his friend took the pony home.

Then we ~~go~~ went on the boat to the Missouri River to Yankton in Dakota. At Yankton two iron horse cars waited to take us to St. Louis.

I was very frightened on the iron horse. So ~~are~~ were the small children. Most of all when the white man's houses began to move away from us. And the long poles of the tele-graph moved, also. I was afraid to sleep on the iron horse. It made louder noises than a grizzly bear. Me and Red Road took turns. One sleeps. One watches. One morning we woke to find that the moon was far behind us when it had been in front the night before. I was ter-ri-fied. Could white people move the moon? If so, they could for sure kill us all. How far were we going? I told Red Road we would fall off the earth. But in the day time some of the older boys sang songs and the little children who were crying got quiet. The songs made them think of home.

Soon we saw houses of the white people. They were so big! They must be very rich. With my people you can tell how rich someone is by how many poles are in the tipi. But these houses did not even need poles! They were so high! Mrs. Mather said they were two stories. To me stories are tales told by our elders. So I thought two elders lived in them. Maybe even a wise woman like my grandmother.

"When we get to St. Louis, you will see buildings that are five times as high," she told me.

"Maybe so you lie," I said.

When we got to St. Louis, I saw she was right. She smiled at me and pointed at the buildings. I was so ashamed, I covered my head with my blanket all the way here.

In St. Louis we had to get off the iron horse and get on another. We walked through a large council house they called Union Sta-tion (I have just looked this word up in my hunting ground book). I peeked through my blanket and saw people pointing at us and staring. I understood enough words to know they had never seen Indians before. So my brother and his friend strutted, acting brave in their blanket Indian clothing. Whiteshield even did some steps in a war dance. The people were afraid. Oh, I thought, he is going to be trouble at school. I knew then he is going to shame our family.

Wicata-wi, Raccoon Moon
February 2

More in-tol-er-a-ble times. The Death Angel has come to us. Horace Watchful Fox died this day. He was of the tribe of Sauk and Fox and was sick for two weeks. They kept him in the in-fir-ma-ry. They say he died from scrof-u-la. They say it taints our blood.

The boys in the shop made him a casket. The teachers wanted to make garlands to put on it. "Let us walk out in the fields and our Mother Earth will give us things to make garlands," Almeda Heavy Hair said. So I went with Almeda, Lena Blackbear, Dora Morning, Ada Fox Catcher, and Frances Bones to gather branches from the ev-er-green, small red berries, and some dry tall weeds that look like what we have on the plains, and wound them into garlands.

All are very sad for Horace Watchful Fox. He worked very hard to learn the white people's ways. We spoke much in sign language of him. For the first time I feel some friendship with the other girls. Then I feel guilty. My true friend is Pretty Eagle. Am I disloyal to her in feeling a kin-ship with a Cheyenne, an Apache, and a Comanche girl? Another Sioux girl? I think not. I think Pretty Eagle would want me to be happy.

February 3

Mr. Captain Pratt wanted to bury Horace Watchful Fox in a white people's cemetery in town. But they want no Indians in their sacred ground. So Mr. Bumpass, who does many jobs here for Mr. Captain Pratt, helped him pick out a spot on school grounds. Mr. Bumpass then dug a big hole in the cold ground. He is many winters and his face looks like he has no good medicine. We call him Old Grump Puss. "We should have our own cemetery," he tells Mr. Captain Pratt. I think why? Does he expect more of us to die? But I do not say these words to anyone.

February 4

Today we buried Horace Watchful Fox. The ground was very hard and cold. I know some of the boys and girls wanted to tear their garments, cut their hair, cover themselves with mud, and slash at their arms because the Death Angel took Horace. But we were made to stand in citizens' clothing, clean and quiet. No fearful wails, but songs of praise to him who giv-eth and him who tak-eth life. I do not know which way is better. We Indians know death. We do not fear it. But I fear the way he was buried, Horace will never find his way to the Great Spirit.

February 5

Some Quaker ladies came today. They brought boxes of books from a tribe called J. B. Lippincott in Phil-a-del-phi-a. They all wear garments of gray. The Gray-Woman-Who-Leads is called Mrs. Longstreth.

Gray-Woman-Who-Leads ~~tells~~ told Mr. Captain Pratt these words: "Thee is undertaking a great work here. Thee will need many things. If thee would receive, thee must ask. Will thee take thy pencil and put down some of the things thee needs very much and the cost?"

I asked Mrs. Camp Bell if it is in-tol-er-a-ble to speak this way. She said no. Only Quakers speak this way. I ask what tribe is this. She said, "It is the tribe of Friends. They are very wealthy."

"Do they have many horses?" I ask. "And large tipis?"

"Yes," she said. "And they have good hearts."

February 6

Again it is the Sabbath, so I have more time to tell of my past.

When we come to this place our iron horse brought us to Gettysburg Junction. Mrs. Mather told us a great battle was fought in Gettysburg in the last big war of the white people.

When they brought us into the council house here many of us stood flat against the wall. Such brightness! Their lights were like so many suns! Someone told how they use whale oil to make this light. I did not know what a whale was, and felt very ignorant. And the whiteness of the walls hurt my eyes. There was much noise, too. Everything echoed. What did the white people have on the ground? Not Mother Earth like inside our tipis. I looked for a way to run.

"Red Road," I yelled. "Save me!"

She was in back of many girls. "Go with them, Little Rose," she called. "They will not hurt you. I am here. I will not let them hurt you."

Then I felt two hands grabbing and pulling me. The girls were taken from the boys. The first thing they made us use was the toi-let. How frightened I was. I thought something from inside its depths might pull me in.

Then we had to bathe. At home we bathe in the river. Never did I see such a bathe place! That was when I first met Belle Rain Water, and she was wearing a white woman's dress. In sign language she told me that she is Hopi. Well,

I thought, Hopi wear white women's dress, maybe so, but I will never do it. Belle Rain Water filled a great pot with kettles full of water. She called me stick girl and made me sit in the big pot. She called it a tub. Then she scrubbed me. I yelled and fought but she held me down. When she let me out she made me put on something called under-where. "A stupid word," I said in sign language. "You know where it goes."

Then I saw the white woman's dress that was waiting for me. I remembered how Red Road told me I would wear a school dress. But I thought they would have one of deer-skin. This was like Belle Rain Water's, only smaller. Belle Rain Water forced it over my head. "This is citizens' cloth-ing," she said. It had many things she called buttons down the back.

"I want deerskin," I yelled. "I am not Hopi! I have too much pride to dress like a white woman!"

Belle Rain Water slapped me and told me to be still while she did up the buttons. I wanted to cry, but would not shame myself. Under the dress she put pet-ti-coats that got in the way when I walked, stock-ings, and heavy shoes with more buttons. I saw other girls being dressed the same way and others like Belle Rain Water, who were helping, car-ried away our blanket clothing.

There was much wailing, much slapping. But the worst was to come.

They brought me to another room and when I saw what they were doing to some small girls, I tried again to run. But they caught me.

They were cutting off their hair. Short. Up to their ears, so the girls looked ugly. Long, shiny braids were piled on the floor. I was so proud of my hair. With my people you cut your hair when you mourn the death of a loved one. If I let them cut my hair surely someone I loved would die! My grandfather? I screamed, but they sat me down hard in the chair and began cutting.

Never will I forget the sound of the scissor, the feel of it when I no longer had braids down my back. A deep loss came over me. My braids gave me comfort, strength. Now my head felt light, as if it might fall off.

At supper that first night no one ate. Stiff in our new clothes, itching from the under-where, mourning the loss of our hair and the blanket Indian clothing they had taken out to burn, we cried, until we were scolded and sent to sleep in the white people's beds, which were high off the floor.

I feared to move, or I would fall. In the room with me

were Almeda Heavy Air and Frances Bones. Both came here before me and were used to scratchy under-where.

"You will get used to it," they told me in sign language. "Do not cry, little Sioux girl. We are your friends."

I did not answer. I wanted no friends who got used to short hair and under-where that scratched, shoes with so many buttons you could never get them on fast if your village was raided. I wanted my soft moccasins. I wanted my deerskin dress and old blanket. I wanted Pretty Eagle. I cried myself to sleep.

The next day they made us pick new names. Names were carved on the boards that are black. They made us go in front of the class and pick up a long stick and point to a name we liked. We could not read the names, so we just pointed.

When my turn came, I asked Mrs. Mary, who came to our class to watch, "Why must I take a new name? I have a name, Little Rose."

"Your old names are hard to say," she tells it.

"Little Rose is not hard to say."

"They tie you to your savage past."

"My past is not savage," I told her.

"You are Sioux. Your people killed Custer."

My under-where is itching me all this time. I feel silly in my citizens' clothes. I trip on the skirts when I walk. I am angry. "My people did not do this thing," I tell her. "That was the Cheyenne and the Oglala Sioux. Spotted Tail kept our people at peace. My people have been at peace with the white man."

Then Mrs. Camp Bell told me not to be dis-re-spect-ful. And to pick a name. So I did, for Mrs. Camp Bell. So now I am Nannie Little Rose. And now I am here. And I have learned to wear this citizens' clothing and write their words. But I will never forget my past. And I did not kill Custer.

February 7

I left off my under-where this morning. So did all the girls in my dormitory. They say Belle Rain Water started this and the older girls do it every Monday. No one knows, but it is a secret way of breaking the rules. It feels good. Not just not being scratched. But breaking the rules.

February 8

This day I saw my brother's class in the yard. They all wore uniforms. They look very scratchy and tight. I did not see my brother's face, but I know what look he is wearing. He will not stay here long if he has to wear such clothes.

February 9

In sewing we learned to make new dresses. Mine is blue and white. Miss Chipmunk says our new dresses are for spring. I sat thinking of my deerskin dress at home with the flounce and the pony beadwork. I remembered how I cured and softened the deerskin for my good dress, then sewed it with buffalo sinew. What would Miss Chipmunk say if I told her I miss my dress? I miss my blanket. I miss my people. And my grandmother's dogs. It comes to me that not only have I not found a brave act to do, but I am not being brave. I do not care. I miss my hair most of all.

February 10

We have a Cree girl here. I talked to her in sewing class. She does not know much English yet, but when Miss Chipmunk was not looking we spoke with our hands.

Her name is Fanny Leaping Water. She said she is a Plains Cree. They have been friendly to the white man and are intelligent. Their enemies are the Blackfeet. But now they all have sufferings and so good words pass between them and the Blackfeet. She says their muskrat and rabbits are most all gone. They need food. They have sold most all their land, ponies, and robes to get food. They say now they fight before they starve.

"Are your people starving?" she asks.

I say yes. "Even though this time of the month our men will go on the beef hunt."

"Beef hunt?" She looks confused because she knows the buffalo are gone.

I tell her that every month cattle are brought to Rosebud Reservation by the white people and let loose, so the young boys can shoot them. The young boys take much pleasure from this hunt. But it is no hunt worthy of the name. Afterward the carcasses are butchered by women and old men. This is how my people get their meat now, not in the old honorable way. We take what is allowed to us by the white man. It is never enough. "And once a year we have *wakpamni* week, when they give us cloth, flannel, and linsey. And blankets."

"You said you wore deerskin at home," Fanny says.

I explain how always, somehow my father hunted down deer so we could cure the skin in our old way. Many of our people don't bother anymore. They take cloth from the white man. But in our family we refuse this cloth. It is a matter of honor.

"My people would not refuse it," she said.

I think her people are worse poor than mine, maybe so.

February 21

I have been very sick. I have lain on a pallet in the in-fir-ma-ry for near two weeks. Coughing, fever. At first I feared I had scrofula and would die like Horace Watchful Fox. My head pounded like drums. I could not eat. Two other girls, Frances Bones and Ada Fox Catcher, had the sickness, too.

They kept trying to feed us soup. The doctor and nurse were very worried. The nurse stayed all night with us. I dreamed that I was home. In my dreams I saw my grand-mother. She was burning sacred tobacco and praying for me. I asked the nurse to let me go home, so I could have my grandmother's tea and the soup she cooks with bones.

"You are better here with our medicines," the nurse said.

But I knew my grandmother's medicine was stronger. It was so strong that she came to me in my dream, across many miles. She told me I will soon be well. That I should be kind to my brother because he is suffering much. And that Pretty Eagle will soon be with me. I am sure her prayers and sacred tobacco she burned made us all well, not the white people's medicine.

I thought much about Pretty Eagle, and it gave me great joy. Soon she will be here, Grandmother said. She must have recovered from her fainting sickness.

We heard that a boy in the in-fir-ma-ry died. His name was Dickens. He was Northern Arapahoe. He had new-monia. (I am too tired to look up the right spell of it.) Many of the teachers cried. Because Dickens was very favored. He was the son of Sharp Nose, the second chief of his tribe. There is much mourning.

February 22

Today is a holiday. The birthday of the white people's great father, George Wash-ing-ton. Gray Beard told us about the Boston tea party. The Mericans dressed like Indians and threw all the tea in the water. Then the English king got very angry and sat for a long time. Then he told his soldiers, go and fight those Mericans. Bring me their scalps. So his warriors went out and there was a rev-o-lu-tion. Wash-ing-ton was a great chief of the Mericans. The war lasted eight years and the soldiers of the king lost their scalps and the Mericans won and made Wash-ing-ton their great father because he could not tell a lie.

February 24

Elkannah, a Cheyenne boy, died today of pneu-mo-ni-a. We have a school band now. The first time it played was to take Elkannah to the grave. It played the Dead March. Too many Indian children are dying. We are filling up our cemetery. There is fear among us. Old Grump Puss is digging many graves. Will this place kill us all?

February 25

A letter has come to our school from the agent for the Osage Indians. Our teachers read it to all the classes. The agent writes that this winter measles and the spotted sickness killed many of the Osage. He says he will not bring any children this spring. They are sickly. We are sad for the Osage children. It seems many tribes besides ours have great trouble.

February 26

Today a doctor comes from Mary-land. His name is Dr. William Osler. And Mr. Captain Pratt says he is very important at Johns Hopkins Uni-ver-si-ty. We must all see this doctor to make certain we do not have a dreadful sickness. It is called tu-ber-cu-lo-sis. I do not have it. Only one boy, George Kills Plenty, a Sioux, has it. They have taken him away.

February 27

Today, after Sunday school, we were allowed to skate on the hard water in the meadow below the school. The teachers wanted to teach us how. But we knew how. We taught them our ice game. Some of the boys carved cedar tops and kept them spinning on the ice for a long time. The teachers much liked the game and laughed and clapped.

February 28

I look always for my spirit helper. If I could find one, I would know what brave act to do. It would tell me. Last night I saw a skunk outside in the dark. The night before I heard an owl. I called out the window to both, but they did not answer. What am I to do? How can I make my people proud of me? Maybe so, I have not been pure enough for a spirit helper. I should fast and go without water to become pure.

Ista-wicayazan-wi, Eyes-Them-Suffer Moon
March 1

I have tried to fast. But when I did not eat two meals, they sent me to the doctor. He looked in my mouth and ears. How silly! He asked me where I hurt. I said I had no hurt, that my people do not eat three times a day but whenever they are hungry. And I am not hungry. How could I say I must fast to find my spirit helper? He said I must eat or stay in the infirmary. So I ate. I was very hungry and they had good meat and potatoes for supper. Also choc-o-late cake. I had two pieces. How can I ever be pure enough to find my spirit helper when I love choc-o-late cake so?

March 2

Today eleven Ponca and Nez Percé children crossed the small wooden bridge that leads to the main yard. We all ran to the windows of our classroom to see. They just stood on the cold parade ground, looking very afraid. They are so small! How different they are from us! They are blanket Indians. Did we look so sad and small when we got here?

Mrs. Camp Bell tells it that before we have another moon, eight Sauk and Fox children are coming. I wait for them to tell us more Sioux are coming. I wait for my friend Pretty Eagle.

March 3

We have one of the Nez Percé boys in our classroom. He cannot speak the white man's language. His name is Talks With Bears. Today he took the name Albert. Mrs. Camp Bell gave him books. *Webb's First Reader* and *Franklin's Arithmetic*. She asked me to picture teach him in back of the class. This is to show him pictures and give him the names of what is in them. He was so frightened, his hands shook.

I saw that his suit was too big and very poor. It is from the piles of clothing Mr. Captain Pratt gave out when we first came here. All the boys' suits from that pile were poor. You could push your finger through the cloth. At that time Mr. Captain Pratt sent a letter to his chief in Wash-ing-ton and said he needed stronger clothing. And if he did not get it he would take ex-tra-or-di-nar-y means. It seems that white men cheat other white men just as they cheat the Indians. Mr. Captain Pratt had to journey to Philadelphia to get more clothing.

In sign language I told Talks With Bears I would ask for cloth and, if my teacher says yes, I will make him a new suit in sewing class. He smiled. His hands stopped shaking.

March 4

I saw Red Road today! We have a new class now. It is called art. Red Road asked Professor Little if she could join the class and learn to draw. I know Red Road can draw better than anybody. She ~~teaches~~ taught me to paint on deerskin. The professor said yes, come join us. We call him Chalk Man. Red Road sat down at a desk and smiled at me. Later when we stood at our ea-sels she told me she came to see what art the white man teaches. "And also, I do not see you much," she said. "This is the one class I can take and see you."

Chalk Man asked us to draw what we remember from home. I drew Grandmother's dogs, but they came out not good. One boy drew a buffalo hunt. Red Road made a drawing of the Sun Dance. The Chalk Man said my dogs were good. He said Red Road's picture was beautiful. Belle Rain Water, the Hopi girl who lives across the hall, made a scalping party. She told Chalk Man his scalp was on one of the brave's lances. Chalk Man said she had much to learn in art. Then she made a face at me and he scolded her for it. I wish this class would happen more than one day a week. It is the only time I get to see Red Road.

March 7

I know now that Belle Rain Water is my enemy. Is it because Chalk Man praised my work and not hers?

Yesterday was the Sabbath. We had in-spec-tion before Sunday school. The night before Sabbath I looked for my Sunday dress. Almeda Heavy Hair and Frances Bones said that Belle Rain Water borrowed it to see how it was made so she could make one for herself, and promised it back in the morning.

In the morning there was my dress, but it was ripped. I had no other to put on. I failed in-spec-tion. Mrs. Mary scolded and said I should not be like the lazy, dirty, good-for-nothing Sioux. I said we are not lazy. I told her the white man had promised us our land for as long as the grass grows and the water runs. That on our land we had sweet grass, clear water, buffalo, and silvery sage. That we grew corn and wheat.

"You are Sioux," she told me back. "You come from the Badlands."

I told her the Badlands are in the plateaus in the territory known as Colorado. As well as the Dakotas. "The bad lands are what the white man gave us in return for taking our land," I told her.

"You will be punished," she said. "Not for the tear in your dress, but for your im-pu-dence."

All the time Belle Rain Water is standing there smiling. What is this im-pu-dence? I asked Almeda Heavy Hair. She said it was the bad way I spoke to Mrs. Mary. I do not think I should be punished for telling her all the places the Badlands are and what the land is the whites gave to us. But I was made to study extra religion and not allowed my free time yesterday. Then I think I should not have spoken such words to Mrs. Mary, maybe so. At home the loud girl is a cause for frowning. I must not allow a bad report to go to my people.

March 9

My brother is in trouble again. He has stolen some meat from the kitchen. I was called out of sewing class to the office of Mr. Captain Pratt. My brother was there. He looked very angry. But Mr. Captain Pratt was more so.

My brother would not speak to Mr. Captain Pratt. I was asked to act as A-Friend-To-Go-Between-Us and ask in our language why my brother took the meat.

"Why did you do this thing? You have made the Captain very angry."

"I wanted to cook the meat in our way," he said. "I wanted to roast it in the ashes."

I feel sad to hear this. I know my brother is bad. I also know he is suffering. He wants to go home and be an Indian warrior. But there is no more place for Indian warriors. I wish my father had not made him count coup. I wish my father did not still wear his chief's clothing. Must we be far from someone to see they have done wrong?

I see now that my father has made my brother think there is still a place for him in the old Sioux world, when there is none. It is as Gray Beard, our history teacher, said in class yesterday: the Sioux people have been conquered for near ten winters now.

I did not say this to Mr. Captain Pratt. Only I told him how my brother longed for meat cooked as we cook it. Mr. Captain Pratt spoke no words for a while, then said he could not have stealing at the school. And my brother must spend two days in the guardhouse.

March 11

Today Miss Chipmunk said I could make a suit for Albert Talks With Bears. She got some good cloth and helped me cut it. Then she said that because the dresses for ourselves were finished, we should all start pro-jects for poor children.

We could make aprons for the colored children in the South, she said. Or quilts for a school in a land across the water called Ja-pan. Everyone was very excited to pick a pro-ject. They had a council meeting and voted to make aprons for the colored children in the South who are very poor. Frances Bones said she would help me with Albert's suit. It is easy to pick a pro-ject. I wish so it would be easy to pick an act of bravery.

I think Miss Monk has a kind heart. I think I will not call her Miss Chipmunk anymore.

March 13, Sabbath

The Sauk and Fox children came today. They look very sad and poor. Miss Monk said it would be good if we made dresses and suits for them before we make aprons for the colored children in the South. Everyone agreed. Frances Bones and I still work on Albert's suit. She wishes to be friends with me. But I hold part of myself closed, as with the other girls. I feel dis-loy-al to Pretty Eagle if I give all of myself to another friend.

March 15

Last night around night-middle-made, we all woke. From outside the windows there was a great wailing. Lights went on in the dormitories. Everyone went to the windows. We looked out to the yard. There was Mr. Captain Pratt and his woman and one of the Sauk and Fox boys. He was wailing as if someone in his tribe had died.

Word went around quickly, like fire. The boy would not allow his hair to be cut. He took a knife and cut his own hair, then went out in the yard to wail.

I could not close my eyes after. Neither could Frances

Bones and Almeda Heavy Hair. They wished to talk, so we did, in sign language. I wanted so much to give more of myself to these girls. Both are kind to me. But I still hold back and wait for Pretty Eagle. I am sure they think I am having my nose in the air because I speak better in the white people's tongue then they do and am often favored.

March 16

Today was fine and warm and sunny. For a while they let us out to watch our school band march. There are so many boys in the band. And though they make them play white people's songs, they do well. The songs are nice, but I long for the sounds of our flutes and drums that seem to bring the music from the plains and hills.

There was a special guest. Her name was Mrs. Walter Baker. She is a very important white woman who owns Baker Chocolate Company. She brought some chocolate for us. Never have I had something that tasted so good. She told Mr. Captain Pratt she will give money to buy more music makers for the school band. I hope this chocolate woman comes again.

March 17

Last night I dreamed my brother was in the band. I wish Grandmother was here to teach me what my dream means. In it my brother was at the head of all the marchers, holding a big stick and leading them.

I asked permission to see my brother today. It was given. "Why don't you go in the band?" I asked him. "I dreamed you went in the band and you led them all."

"Women's dreams are worth nothing," my brother said.

"And what of our grandmother?"

His eyes walk away from me. "I do not wish to make the white people's music."

March 18

After supper tonight we were all brought into the sitting room for some en·ter·tain·ment. A man came who did magic. He had a rabbit and made it disappear. What happened to the rabbit? With my people all animals have spirits. If he killed the rabbit to use its skin, he should have thanked it first.

He took flowers out from under a cloth. When he was finished, Mr. Captain Pratt asked him to tell us how he did his tricks. I see that the rabbit was still alive. Mr. Captain Pratt told us that there is no magic. He said, "All the super-natural things done by Indian medicine men can be explained and are not magic at all."

But I know our medicine man can do magic. Didn't he pray and sing over Grandfather when he had the spotted sickness? And make him better?

March 29

No time to write in my book for many suns. For a good reason. Haye! Haye! Thanks be! Pretty Eagle has come!

It was most not expected. She came on the 19 day of March with two other Sioux girls and the Indian agent from Rosebud. The other girls are White Whirlwind and Brave Killer.

"I don't know where we will put them," Mrs. Camp Bell said. "All the dormitories are not yet finished. Captain Pratt has asked if any girls will make the sacrifice of having another girl in their room."

I did not understand how taking in a friend can be a sacrifice. I spoke up. I said if Frances Bones and Almeda Heavy Hair agree, I would take Pretty Eagle in our room. "She is my friend from home," I said. "I will make her my pro-ject. I will set my mind to the task."

Almeda and Frances both said it was good to do this. Then other girls said they would take in White Whirlwind and Brave Killer. The teachers had a new bed ~~bring~~ brought to our room.

When I first saw Pretty Eagle, I ran. Right across the yard to Mr. Captain Pratt's office. We embraced. Oh, I felt how thin she is. Her bones come through her skin. And she looked so strange in her blanket clothing.

After we hugged we stood back and looked at each other. She touched my short hair and her eyes grew sad. "You wrote about your braids in the letter to your father," she said. "But I still do not understand why."

"I do not know why," I told her. "It must be done."

We were speaking in our language. This is forbidden in school. I looked at Mr. Captain Pratt. He nodded. "You may take Pretty Eagle to your room," he said. "Today you may converse in your language, but after today you must try and teach her English. You may have the day off, to find her citizens' clothing and have her hair cut."

I promised and we walked across the yard. I dreaded the moment Pretty Eagle would have to have her beautiful, long hair cut. I have gotten used to mine, but never will I get used to hers chopped off. I did not say this to her.

I saw her looking at my citizens' clothing. More sadness came in her eyes. She was wearing her dress with shells on the yoke. And her shawl with the beaded hem. She looked so beautiful!

"They make us dress so," I told her. "They take our blanket clothing. Did my father not tell you also that you should not wear your good things?"

She nodded. "I wear them anyway."

"They will take them from you."

Only she smiles then. "I am here, am I not? I know what to expect. It is worth the sacrifice. Even my hair, to be with you."

How are things at home? I asked her. Her eyes walked away from me.

The same, she said. "We are still poor. There is no hunting. The ground is not good. Your grandmother is glad to know you have recovered from your illness. Your mother says, why do you write to your father only, and not to her?"

At home we fought, I reminded her. She had no good words for me. Now she wants me to write?

We both laughed. It was good to hear her laugh. Then Pretty Eagle told me how guilty my mother felt because her father was one of the chiefs who signed away our land. And how unworthy, because, though Sioux men often take more than one wife, my father had wanted Red Road, who was so much younger and prettier.

"She is unhappy with herself," Pretty Eagle said. "So she strikes out at you, her daughter, because you have your whole life ahead of you. You are young. And still have a chance to do things right."

Oh, I am so happy Pretty Eagle is here! I know things will be better for me now. I have my true friend. Perhaps she can help me find my spirit helper. I showed her how to use the toilet. I searched the whole school for a good dress for her. One of the teachers gave me a dress she no longer uses. Pretty Eagle is very frightened. I held her hand while they cut her hair. When it was chopped short, Pretty Eagle shook her head and only she laughed. "It feels so light," she said. "I think I will like it."

I sat next to her in the dining hall and showed her how to use a fork and knife. She is learning fast. For eleven suns now I have been taking care of Pretty Eagle. Mrs. Camp Bell said she was very proud of me. And Almeda Heavy Hair and Frances Bones. In class Belle Rain Water made a face. I think she will make more trouble for me. But I have no time to think of that now.

Magaksica-agli-wi, Ducks-Together-Come Moon
April 4

Pretty Eagle has taken a name. It is Lucy.

April 7

We lighted the council fire between us in our room last night before we lay on our pallets — me, Almeda Heavy Hair, Frances Bones, and Pretty Eagle. They much like to hear what Pretty Eagle has to say because she just came from a reservation. Since Almeda has been teaching Frances Lakota words, we could all speak in Lakota. How should we know that Belle Rain Water was outside our door, listening? She told Mrs. Mary we were speaking in Lakota, and since this is forbidden, we were punished. For two weeks we are not allowed to have our door closed. Worst part yet is that Mrs. Mary made Belle in charge. She is to spy on us and report if we speak in Lakota. I hate Belle Rain Water.

April 14

I have much ne-glect-ed my little book. Frances and I have finished the suit for Albert Talks With Bears. He is full of himself now that he is looking good. He walks like a true brave and not like a whipped dog. Another boy helps him in class now so I can help Pretty Eagle.

April 15

Pretty Eagle has told me more of home. More white people are coming and spoiling what hunting is left. She said my father still wears his chief's shirt, and now he speaks of the return of the buffalo. This gives me much worry. Most of us know the buffalo will never return. I pray my father is not living in his mind in The-Time-That-Was-Before. My grandmother is well. She did much visiting from tipi to tipi this winter. Grandfather has trouble walking. I must pray for him. She said the white people make claims against the an-nu-i-ties our people got for the land.

It is spring now where we come from. But I wonder if the land smiles again, if the cottonwood trees have large clusters of pods, if the young grapevines are growing, if the sweet grass is plentiful in the meadows. I wonder if the water runs clear and cold. And if the tiny birds we call *skibibila* chirp all around. What can we do to help our people? I asked Pretty Eagle. Only she smiles and says, "I am trying." What does that mean? How can she, a girl like me, help our people here in the land of Penn-syl-va-ni-a?

April 16

Pretty Eagle fainted this day. Good that it was in Mrs. Camp Bell's class. I was allowed to go with her to the infirmary. They kept her there. I am much worried about her.

April 17

Pretty Eagle is back from the infirmary. "You still have the fainting sickness," I told her. "You should not have come here to school."

I was much angry with her. "They will send you home," I scolded. "Mr. Captain Pratt has enough dying this winter past." More I was feeling guilty that she came here to be with me when she is sick.

She tells me it is not the fainting sickness. She tells me she has learned to have a trance, like my grandmother.

I asked her if she prayed to get this trance.

She says yes. But she must practice more, she tells it, so she can better help our people. Then she says that when she has a trance I must tell everyone she gets fainting spells. I must never tell them it is a trance.

"So then, all those fainting spells you had at home were trances?" I ask.

Only she smiles, and says yes. I ask if our people know this. Just her mother and father, she says. "And your grandmother, who has been teaching me the Powers. Your grandmother says I have good medicine."

Oh, I am jealous! My grandmother teaching Pretty Eagle, saying she has good medicine. And all the while my grandmother knowing I wanted to do this, and telling me, wait, wait, until you get older. Pretty Eagle is my age! Was grandmother just being kind to me?

I asked Pretty Eagle if she had a spirit helper.

She says yes. At home she purified herself. And fasted. And went to the plains alone. All the things I wanted to do. Her spirit helper is the eagle. He came to her when she was alone on the plains and told her the Indians and the buffalo are the same. The buffalo were given to us by the

Spirit of the Earth. Now they are gone. Soon we will be gone, unless we children do not forget our people and our ways.

Then he gave her a vision. He told her to come here to show the children it is not wrong to be here, to learn the ways of the white man. Learn their songs, their history, their artwork, their religion, so we can make our way in the world, but never forget our own way. Her spirit helper told her she would leave her mark here. How, she does not know.

A vision! Pretty Eagle had a vision! Always I thought someday I would grow up and have visions. Like my grandmother!

But how could I be jealous? She is my dear friend. Again she made me promise never to tell them here that she has trances. Or they will send her back, for sure. They will fear her. Better they think she has the fainting sickness. Then she says I must help her. She cannot do what she was sent to do, without my help.

"Will you do this for me?" she asks.

Yes. But oh, how small I felt. Like a mouse, chased into a hole by an eagle. How unworthy next to Pretty Eagle.

"And you promise never to let them know I have trances? No matter what happens?"

I promised. But oh, I was jealous.

April 18

Every month I have written a letter home to my father. When Mrs. Camp Bell ~~learn~~ learned that never have I written to my mother, she made me write the letter today in class.

Here is my letter, which I will copy into my diary:

Dear Mother:

I know some agent or trader at Rosebud will read this to you as they have read my letters to Father. I am well. Winter here has been some bad but not as bad as at home. When first I came here I missed home very much. Now I am more at home here. But I have not turned my face from my people. Each day I look in the white people's mirror in the hall and see that I have not lost my face.

My teachers say I am doing well in school. I am not so good in arithmetic, but am im-proving. I am learn-ing history and geography. Also cooking and sewing. I am already on my fourth reading book. Also I am help-ing to teach Pretty Eagle, who came to us this month. She tells me Grandfather is not walking so good. Tell him Little Rose sends much love and prays for him. I pray to the Sioux spirits and to the white people's god. So he should be better two times as fast. I think I am get-ting a good education. And when I come home I will be able to help our people.

In sewing class we are making new dresses for the summer time. Miss Monk, who teaches us sewing, said she will send the best ones to the land of Philadelphia to the State Fair. This is like our Sun Dance, only nobody dances. Maybe so I will win a prize.

Tell Grandmother I love her very much. And I miss her dogs.

With fond love, I am your af-fec-tion-ate daughter, Nannie Little Rose.

I must now put out the light.

April 19

Pretty Eagle is better and back in class. You would never know she fainted. She has more strength than any of us. I have only two classes with her, English and sewing. In all other classes she is not with me. She is just learning to write. I am teaching her English. Some days I spend extra time doing this. So Mrs. Camp Bell writes a note. And I do not have to go to cooking. Frances Bones tells me that Woman-Who-Screams-A-Lot is angry I do not come. So is Belle Rain Water, because they have made her do my work. But it is im-por-tant that I teach Pretty Eagle to speak En-glish, so she can do what the spirits sent her here to do. She learns fast.

April 20

Many of the older boys are working hard in the fields after school. They are plant-ing and hoe-ing. Potatoes, wheat, oats, rye. They let the girls work in a small ve-ge-ta-ble garden. I am growing rows of beans. It made me know how I miss Mother Earth.

April 22

Two days of rain. No one can go outside. The rain runs off the outside pipes. The boys' dormitory did not leak.

They put in a new pipe before the rains come. It is called terra-cotta. We all have colds. Much sneezing. I hope Pretty Eagle does not get sick.

April 24

Back to my kitchen duties. Woman-Who-Screams-A-Lot says, "Where were you? Someone else had to do your work. You are a sloucher."

I do not know what this sloucher is. I told her I was teaching Pretty Eagle English.

"Well," she said. "Belle Rain Water has been doing your work for you. Now you can do the work for others. You can scrub everyone's pots when they are finished cooking."

Again my hands are sore. I hate Woman-Who-Screams-A-Lot. I saw a mouse in the kitchen today. I wish it would bite her.

April 27

I have been so tired, I have not had time to write for two suns. In sewing we are working on our summer dresses.

I am making mine with a flounce at the bottom. When I told Miss Monk I wanted to do pony beadwork, she said, "Why don't you do em-broi-dery?" I know now, because of what Pretty Eagle told me, that this is a way to make me forget about pony beadwork. So I learned embroidery, but in my mind I went over the way to do pony beadwork.

My hands hurt so. I am still scrubbing pots in the kitchen. And doing embroidery on the flounce of my dress. Belle Rain Water says her dress will win the prize. It is yellow. I do not like the sleeves. Mine is white. I also am trying still to teach Pretty Eagle English.

April 30

I saw the mouse in the kitchen again today. After all had left and I was scrubbing the pots, it came out of a hole in the wall. I fed it some old bread. It ate the bread up fast and looked at me with eyes that are bright and clear. With my people we believe that all things have a spirit. A war club has a spirit. A prairie dog has two spirits. Birds, insects, and reptiles have spirits. Even a mouse. While I scrubbed my pots, the mouse visited with me. He is not afraid.

Canwape-ton-wi, Tree-Leaves-Potent Moon
May 1

My brother has done a brave deed. A man came to the gate yesterday. Many times men come to the gate, seeking food or water. On the reservation when strangers come, we feed them. They smoke with the chiefs. It is very important to share what you have. Even if you have only a small amount of cornmeal. Here they call the visitors tramps. You must know a special word to get through the gate and tramps do not know it so they are not let inside.

This tramp crawled over the wall and stole wood. My brother saw him and grabbed of him and ~~brings~~ brought him to the guardhouse. My brother was much praised for his bravery.

"I am a warrior," he told Mr. Captain Pratt.

I am much proud of him. But also jealous. I have not yet done a brave deed to bring honor to my people.

May 3

Today I finished the embroidery on the flounce of my dress. I think it is very pretty. I am still washing pots in the kitchen. I want to make pie and pudd-ing. Woman-Who-Screams-A-Lot says no. Again I saw my mouse friend and fed him after all left. Pretty Eagle is learning English very good. Since she is at the beginning of her learning here, she is in classes with small girls. She does not mind this. Because she is so pretty and nice, many of the little girls make friends with her. She fusses over them and they all wish to be like her. I think she is teaching them on the sly to remember their old ways. I think she is doing what she was sent here to do, maybe so.

May 5

In geography today Gray Beard told us that the world is round, and whirls around the sun. I feel as if everything I am is leaving me, hearing this. All my training is in the air if this is true. If we whirl around the sun, why do we not feel the spinning? If we whirl around the sun, why are there days there is no sun? I think Gray Beard lies.

I told my friend the mouse this today when we were alone again in the kitchen. I think he understands.

May 8

Last night I dreamed about my friend the mouse. In my dream he spoke to me. He said, "What does it matter if the earth whirls around the sun?" He said, "You were taught that the earth is flat. As long as we and our loved ones have enough to eat and a place to stay warm, it does not matter if the earth is round or flat." He said, "What is important is that you know what you believe. Stay on the path of what you know."

When I awoke, a thought came into my head. Maybe so, my friend the mouse is my spirit helper.

Yes, I know. Boys on the reservation have coyotes, bears, wolves, all great and powerful. Pretty Eagle has an eagle. I get a mouse. I think it is because my spirit is not pure. I am all the time wanting to be the best, wanting to do a brave act. I am boastful, like my brother. I will ask Red Road if it is possible for the mouse to be my spirit helper. I would like to ask Pretty Eagle, but I am ashamed. She has such good medicine and I have none.

May 9

In art class I asked Red Road if she thinks the mouse can be my spirit helper. She said yes. In this place I will find no coyotes or wolves or bears. I must take what I can get. Then I asked myself: What have I done to earn a spirit helper? Nothing. Yet the little mouse came and spoke to me in my dream. I am grateful for him.

May 13

I have been leaving bread for my little mouse every night. Yesterday he came out of his hole in the middle of class and all saw him. Woman-Who-Screams-A-Lot screamed more than ever. "I will not have a mouse in my kitchen!" she said. "Someone must kill him."

May 14

More and more I am seeing how the little girls gather around Pretty Eagle. In the yard during rec-re-a-tion, she plays ball with them. She laughs with them. She has a good spirit and they are drawn to her. I see smiles on many faces where I have not seen them before.

Yesterday after everyone left, Belle Rain Water came back into the kitchen. She had taken off her apron and forgotten it. She saw my little mouse eating the bread I put down for him.

"You are feeding him," she said.

.I did not dare tell her he is my spirit helper. I think now she will tell Woman-Who-Screams-A-Lot. What should I do? Feed him no more so he does not come? I must think on the matter.

May 15

Again my mouse spirit helper came to me in my dream. He told me he would not be with me for long, in body. But in spirit he would always be with me. He told me I would soon find my one brave act. "What will it be?" I asked. He said part of the bravery is in knowing when I am needed. In stepping forth at the right time. "How will I know the right time?" I asked him. He said I will know, not to worry.

Today Belle Rain Water told Woman-Who-Screams-A-

Lot I was feeding the mouse. She scolded me. "He won't be around long," she said. "Whichever one of you kills him will not have to wash pots for a month."

But she had her mind on another path. Today we must learn to make bread, she said. "Indians do not know how to work with yeast. This is why Captain Pratt has a white man as baker. Let us see if you can prove us all wrong."

So we were all set to making bread. At home I have made *teepsinna*, turnips, and *wasna*, pounded sun-dried meat mixed with dried cherries. I have cooked the meat from the deer and buffalo. I have made cornmeal cakes.

I kneaded my bread, like all the others. Across the table from me I see that Belle Rain Water is kneading too hard. But I said no words to her. Then we covered the bread with a piece of cloth and left it to rise.

Trouble now. My bread rose. So did all the others'. When Woman-Who-Screams-A-Lot took the cloth from Belle Rain Water's, we saw it did not.

"She put a spell on my bread," Belle said of me. "Because I told of her feeding the mouse. She is a witch! My people know there are witches," she said.

Woman-Who-Screams-A-Lot said she does not believe in witches. She set Belle to washing pots. I felt gladness at first. Then worry. Pretty Eagle told me later that Hopis learn secret powers and can make you very sick if they choose. I am sure Belle will do bad to me.

May 16

When I went to cooking class this afternoon, my mouse spirit helper was dead. Belle Rain Water has killed him. She struts around, so proud. I tried to think of what the little mouse said in my dream, that he would not be with me long in body, but in spirit always. It helped some when I buried him in the flower bed outside the kitchen, but not much. I can write no more now.

May 19

For two days I have had no words in me. Now my heart is finding words. Where was I when Belle Rain Water killed my spirit helper? I would wash pots forever if it meant saving him. Today I was so angry, I drove my wooden spoon through the bottom of a jar of turnips. At our table we had no turnips for supper. Everyone likes turnips. I feel bad that I did this thing. Then Pretty Eagle told me my spirit helper was not dead, but has gone somewhere else to help another person. I feel better about that, but I wish he was still here with me.

May 26

For a week now they have taken from us our student lamps, so I could not write. The cry "Fire, fire!" went through the air just after we all went to sleep on May 19. The oil in the tube of a student lamp in one of the boys' rooms blazed high. The table cover and chair burned. Both were thrown out the window. Before it was over we all went out into the night until it was safe to go back inside.

While we were all standing out in the night I saw Pretty Eagle hushing the fears of the little girls. I heard her tell them that fire can be bad and they must always be careful around their lamps. Then she reminded them how fire can be good. How it lights our ceremonial pipes. How it is an honor to carry burning coals on a ceremonial fire stick to make a spirit fire that brings spirits of former friends to give good counsel. She quieted my fears, too, as I listened.

Mrs. Mary said the boy who started the fire with his

lamp was careless. So we were all punished when they took away our lamps.

May 28

Since the days are so warm, some teachers allow us to have class outside. Now that spring is here it is so hard to sit inside all day. I think of home. All the children do. Today we had much excitement. The boys were so tired of school, they wanted to go outside and run. So they thought of a way to have a day off from school. One let the pigs escape.

Pigs were all over the yard. Running and squealing. From under the trees our class saw this and joined in the chasing of the pigs. All afternoon we chased pigs and had a wonderful time. When we were finished we were all full of dirt and laughing. Mr. Captain Pratt thanked us for saving the pigs.

May 30

Mr. Captain Pratt asked who would go with him to Gettysburg to put flowers on the graves of the soldiers who died in the white man's last war. Many went. First we gathered flowers from the grounds to put on the graves. Mr. Captain Pratt was one of the soldiers in this war. He told us how all the white men killed each other.

With my people if a loved one dies, one can become a Spirit Keeper, who keeps the spirit of the dead person on earth for a year. In that year one must pray and mourn. And keep a piece of the loved one's hair and other possessions in a Spirit Bundle. Then you make a Spirit Post from cottonwood and paint on it a face that is the loved one. This post is put in the ground in front of the Spirit Keeper's tipi. A bowl of food must be kept always, for a guest to eat. Guests come and bring gifts. They are put into the bundle. When the Keeper is ready to release the spirit, the post and bundle are held up to the sun and prayers are said. The gifts are given away in the name of the person who has died.

Putting flowers on the graves is nice, too. I think maybe the white people are not so different from us. We both kill many people in war.

Tipsinla-wi, **Prairie-Rice-Like Moon**
June 1

All are very ex-cit-ed. Today we had a postal telling
that our chiefs are coming to visit. Red Cloud and Spotted
Tail. They are on a journey to visit the white people's
father in Wash-ing-ton. They are going to look at our
school.

June 3

Now that the sun shines each day they make us go outside and play. All grass and trees are very green, and there
are flowers blooming all around. Never have I seen so much
green. It makes things cool and nice. These white people
have the best part of the country, maybe so. I am thinking
of the dry, open ground on our reservation, without tree or
shade.

They want us to play games outside. Drop the handker-
chief and blindman's buff. What are we to learn about making our way in the world from such games? At home girls
played marbles. Our marbles are made of small stones. We
played toss and catch with the hooves of deer. We played

the plum-pit game. All these games ~~teach~~ taught us to think and be noble.

June 4

Today Mr. Captain Pratt made a speech in the din-ing room. He said school is almost over for the year and he is most proud of us. He said this summer some children will go home. Others will go on "outings." This means they will work on nearby farms. Or live with Quaker families and help in the house. They will be paid for their work. I would like to do this. The Quakers are a good tribe. Mr. Captain Pratt says soon he will say who will go home and who will stay here and who will go with the Quaker tribe. There is much big talk about this. Red Road and her husband acted as Friends-To-Go-Between-Us and told Mr. Captain Pratt's words to some children who still do not understand the white people's language.

June 6

I am learning phys-i-ol-o-gy. Today I learned that the blood makes all things work in our body. It makes the tears work in our eyes and the wax work in our ears. The blood runs in my veins and makes my heart pump and the blood makes our teeth and our lungs work. And the yellow soft stuff in our heads that we use to think. The blood makes our life.

June 7

Today two things happened in sewing class. Miss Monk sent my dress to the State Fair in Philadelphia. She sent two others. That of Frances Bones and Belle Rain Water. I know Belle will hate me if I win. Then she will do more bad to me. Then just when I am thinking hard of this, Pretty Eagle fainted again. The nurse woman came and they took her to the infirmary. Miss Monk said I could go with her.

June 10

I stayed all the first day with Pretty Eagle in the infirmary. Except for the time I slipped out to pick her some violets. She loves the violets they have here. At fading-time she came out of her trance. When she woke she saw the violets and made a smile and then looked very worried.

"You must not let Mr. Captain Pratt send me home this summer," she says in our language. "I have too much work to do here with the children."

I told her she was doing good work with the children. That because of her, times were easier for them here. The little girls looked happier, and I had heard some of them reminding each other not to forget their Indian names and customs. Then I promised I would beg Mr. Captain Pratt not to send her home this summer. But then I must stay here also and keep watch on her. This means I cannot go on an outing. It is more important that I stay and help Pretty Eagle. She needs me. And I am no longer jealous of her. I am proud to help her.

June 12

Again Mr. Captain Pratt spoke to us today. This time his words were very heavy. He said we must think on what we wish to become.

"Before they are finished at Carlisle, some boys will become silversmiths. Some will be tinsmiths. Some farmers, some raisers of cattle. Some will build houses of brick. Some will be plumbers. Still others will go to the white man's college and learn more. Next year you will con-centrate on what craft you choose."

Then he spoke to the girls: "Some of you will go into home economics, business, teaching, or nursing," he told us. "And some will go on to study more and become missionaries."

I asked Red Road what she wants to be. She smiled and said, "A mother." How can I think of what I want to be now? Not many can. All we can think of is summer.

June 13

Three iron horse carloads of tinware and stovepipe made by boys at this school were shipped to different

Indian agencies in the West this month. This was told to us by Mrs. Camp Bell today. She said we should be very proud.

June 15

In art class today Chalk Man drew angles. "This is an obtuse angle," he told us. Then he drew more angles. Then he pointed to one. "What is this angle?" he asked.

Pretty Eagle has not had many art classes. "Obstinate angle," she said.

All laughed. "I am stupid," Pretty Eagle told me later.

"No," I told her. "You have your own good medicine. You do not need what they teach you here."

June 16

As well as work in the vegetable garden, I work in the flower garden every day. The roses are blooming now. This makes me happy, since my name is Little Rose. Many other flowers are blooming, too. We must not pick them. They are for the rooms of Mr. Captain Pratt and his wife. And for people who come to visit.

But here there are fields of daisies. We pick them for our teachers. I picked the last of the violets for Lucy. She said they make her happy. We both miss the crisp buffalo grass, silvery sage, white poppies, and wild sunflowers we have at home.

June 17

Today Mr. Captain Pratt told us who will be going on outings this summer, and who will be going home. Most of the older boys and girls want to go on outings and earn money. Whiteshield's name is on the list to work with a Quaker family. But he says he does not wish to go. Belle Rain Water and Lena Blackbear are going. So are Almeda Heavy Hair, Maggie Stands Looking, and Frances Bones. My name was on the list to go with a Quaker family. I was so happy! Then I remembered I cannot leave Pretty Eagle! Red Road is not going on an outing. I wonder if it is because she is married. Or because she is needed here. I am needed here also. If Red Road can give up an outing, so can I.

June 18

My heart has been so heavy. What can I do? I can tell no one about Pretty Eagle's trances, but I must not be sent on an outing! I must think what to do.

June 19

I have spoken with Red Road. Last night at fading-time I went to her little house. Her husband was not there and she made me sit and gave me tea. I did not tell Red Road about Pretty Eagle's trances, though I wished I could. I told Red Road I did not feel I could leave Pretty Eagle this summer, that she needs me.

"This is a wonderful chance for you, Little Rose," she said in our language. "You like the Quakers. But if you feel you cannot leave your friend, then I will ask Captain Pratt if you can stay and care for her. Sometimes we must stay where we are needed."

When Red Road said that, it was as if I had a vision! Of course! It came to me then, what my mouse spirit helper told me. How part of bravery is knowing when you are needed, and stepping forth at the right time. Yes, yes! This is my brave act! To care for Pretty Eagle! Because she is doing important work here. Oh, my heart was so glad to find my brave act that I hugged Red Road and thanked her. I told her I wished she had married my father, because she is like a second mother to me, better than my own mother.

She scolded softly then and said I must not say ugly words about my real mother. Then she smiled and said that if she had married my father I would soon be having a little sister or brother. Because she is to have a child.

I hugged her again. I am very happy for her. And I feel a little guilty because I could not tell her about Pretty Eagle's trances. Oh, I did not know how hard it would be to keep a promise to a friend! But we Sioux always keep our word. It is part of our honor.

June 22

There was no time to write for days. No time to think of who is to go where this summer. The whole school is making ready for the visit of our chiefs.

Things had to be scoured and cleaned. Bedding changed. Rooms and washrooms made neat. Flower garden weeded. Fields hoed. Workshops made to show their wares.

Flowers put in the chapel. Porches painted and even hammocks hung.

Then we had to practice a sing. Some boys are picked to make a speech. Our schoolwork is put out so the chiefs can see what we have learned. But most important, our cooking class is to make the food for the guests. Woman-Who-Screams-A-Lot is about to ferment. She says she will cut off our ears if we do not do our best cooking. Lena Blackbear is to make biscuits and roast the meat. Almeda Heavy Hair is to make the sponge cake and gravy. Frances Bones will make the bread. Belle Rain Water will make the custard pie. I am to make the eggs, roast potatoes, and coffee. In between I am watching over Pretty Eagle. She is busy keeping the little ones out of the way. I hope she does not get herself too tired.

June 23

The chiefs came today! Our school band played as they came over the wooden bridge and through the gate. Two young girls gave them flowers. Oh, they looked so fine in their blankets and turkey tails and hats full of feathers. I was so proud. How can our teachers see them and want to change us from what we are? I felt so different from them, in my citizens' clothing. I wanted to wear blanket clothing again. Red Road ran to meet her father, Spotted Tail. I feel so alone. I wish my father had come, too. In his chief's clothing he looks as good as Spotted Tail and Red Cloud. Maybe so.

First the reverend gave a sermon in the chapel. He talked of the as-cen-sion. This is when the Jesus god rose on a great cloud and went to heaven.

Chief Red Cloud asked to speak. "Why God's son came to the world and go away again?" he asked. "Earth not good enough? Why he leave us here to struggle?"

Reverend and Chief Red Cloud had much big talk about this. Sometimes Red Road had to act as A-Friend-To-Go-Between-Us.

After chapel we all went to the dining hall. The chiefs sat in a place of honor with the Indian agents. All of us cook girls waited on the table. They very much enjoyed the supper. Mr. Rice, an Indian agent, said it was a better meal than they got on the iron horse and they paid much for it. We did not charge them anything. Woman-Who-Screams-A-Lot did not cut off our ears.

After supper there were speeches by some of our boys. I was part of the girls in the sing. Then the chiefs went to the workshops, and visited the classrooms. Tomorrow Red Cloud will make a speech. I am very tired.

June 24

This day there is trouble. In the dining hall at breakfast word goes from table to table in soft voices, like wind on the plains.

Chief Spotted Tail is very angry. He does not like the soldier uniforms on the boys. He does not want the boys to become like the white soldiers. He is angry because his younger son, who took the name of Paul, is in the guardhouse. After breakfast the Sioux children went to chapel to hear Red Cloud speak.

"You are all my grandsons and granddaughters," he said in the white people's language. "I am most glad to see you. I went pass through the shops and saw what you can be done. I saw the shoemaker, harness maker, tailor, carpenter, tinner, blacksmith. You see I wear boots which is you make. I see the boys' and girls' quarters and all what you have in rooms and washrooms. Also the girls can washing clothes and sewing. They doing very well and I was very pleased. I like here everything. This is good place.

"I go to schoolrooms and see you can read books and writing. Now this is why we send you here, for to learn white men's way. There is two roads, one is good and the other we call a devil road. Another thing is, you know who do nothing, so any dime not come into his pocket. Be not like that.

"Your teachers are good. You must obey them and obey this man he is keep you here. I am very glad you are all well and doing good, so I can tell to your fathers, mothers, sisters, and brothers. Now you must not be homesick. But you must be happy all the time and trying to learn all you can. This is all. We go to Washington today to meet with pres-i-dent. We stop here again on way home. You must not be sorry when we are gone. We meet again soon."

Then he comes to hug each of us Sioux children. "Little Rose, daughter of White Thunder, your father is proud of you."

It made me happy and sad. Because I wanted to tell him about my brave act. I wanted my father to know.

June 25

The chiefs are gone. Today I saw my brother. He told me that Chief Spotted Tail's son Paul is in the guardhouse because he stabbed a schoolmate in the leg with his jackknife. He said that Red Road explained to her father that his older son, Max, was on the court that put Paul in the guardhouse. But Chief Spotted Tail is still very angry and when he comes back he will take all the Sioux children home.

You lie, I told my brother.

If I lie, he says back, so does Max. Max told him this, and Max's father told Max.

"Mr. Captain Pratt won't let us go," I said. "And I do not wish to go. I wish to stay and learn more so I can help our people."

My brother wants to know how I can help our people. He says I am not a warrior, just a girl.

I told him then the words that I had not yet told myself. "I will become a teacher," I said.

My brother laughed. Then he grew stern and said I was to tell no one about Spotted Tail. Of course I will not. Still, I waited for Red Road to speak to me of the matter. Surely she knows what her father has said. But she spoke no words to me.

June 30

I have not written in my diary. I am very sad because of what my brother said.

Those who will go on outings are packing and going to special classes to learn how to act in the outside world. I am working in the flower garden and sewing a new dress. I have spent some time with Red Road, helping her pack. She and her husband will go home this summer. She says she hopes to be back in fall, after the baby comes. Again I waited for her to give me some words about her father taking back the Sioux children. Almeda Heavy Hair is Sioux and I do not wish her to go home. I know she does not wish to go. And I am not ready to go home. I have not done my brave act yet. But Red Road said no words to ease my heart. It seems we both have secrets we cannot tell each other. And they are like weeds on the path, keeping us from each other.

Canpa-sapa-wi, Choke-Cherry Moon
July 1

Families who are taking children in for summer outings came to pick them up. I said good-bye to Frances Bones, but at the last minute Almeda Heavy Hair was not allowed to go, because Spotted Tail may yet take the Sioux children home. Then Belle Rain Water decided she was not going, either. She told Mr. Captain Pratt she did not wish to be a slave to the stick ladies in gray. They had a council with Mr. Captain Pratt and Ada Fox Catcher went in Belle's place. It turned out the Quaker ladies did not want Belle anyway. They said she was sullen.

So now it is just Almeda Heavy Hair, Pretty Eagle, and me in our room. The school seems very quiet. But I still go to sewing class. We are making very strange dresses. Miss Monk says they are to swim in. We laughed. At home we do not wear clothing to swim. Miss Monk said, "You will see." Today I saw Red Road, and she smiled. She is all packed and ready to go home. But she still said no words to me about her father's decision. I will wait for her to speak of it when she is ready.

July 2

Today my brother told me he asked Mr. Captain Pratt if he could go home for the summer, but was told no. I think Mr. Captain Pratt fears my brother will not come back. I think he is right.

Everyone is very busy making ready for the fourth day of the Choke-Cherry Moon month. This is the day the white people signed their treaty that they no longer wanted to be part of the tribe across the great water. What this means is that every fourth day of the Choke-Cherry Moon month the white people make a lot of food and cakes and play games. Mrs. Camp Bell also told us about the picnic we will have. White people get very excited about eating outside under the sky.

July 3

Today we were helping to set up tables under the trees for the picnic tomorrow. Then one of the boys saw a blanket Indian boy coming across the wooden bridge. He wore only leggings and white man's shoes. Everyone ran to meet him. He was very near dead and in need of water. His name is Wapka, First-Who-Spies-The-Enemy. He is Potawatomi, from the land of Mich-i-gan. He was in school in that land, but always running away. He said he has a friend here who wrote to him of our school and how good it is. So he walked here all the way.

July 4

All morning many girls helped Woman-Who-Screams-A-Lot in the kitchen, making the feast for the fourth day of the Choke-Cherry Moon month. I cut the potatoes for the salad. I also helped make ice cream. Never have I tasted anything so good!

This night we ate outside on the tables under the trees. All the teachers are happy. We had a sing and played games. Mr. Captain Pratt asked some of the boys to help him set off firecrackers. My brother helped with this. It is the only time I have seen him happy since he has been here. We stayed up very late. The firecrackers were like comets in the sky.

After it was over Red Road told me she and her husband have been asked by Mr. Captain Pratt to return in fall as Friends-To-Go-Between-Us because many new children will be coming. I was most glad to hear this.

July 5

Today Mr. Captain Pratt made a speech at breakfast. He said all who stay here in the summer will be going on trips to different places. Also there will be a summer camp near a place called Tagg's Run, where students will live in tents, pick berries, and hunt and fish.

"This is something to get excited about?" I heard Belle Rain Water mumble. I think she is getting meaner every day.

Mr. Captain Pratt had a list of projects, too. He said we should all pick a project for the summer. He said if we do not go to the camp the girls can swim in the afternoon in the millrace, the canal in the meadow below the school. The boys can swim in the natural limestone cave on the Conodoguinit Creek. Belle Rain Water said she will never wear a dress to swim.

July 7

This day at fading-time we gathered under the trees in the yard to hear the tale of Wapka, who now calls himself Samuel. His father is a Frenchman. His mother is a Potawatomi. He earned his way here by being A-Friend-To-Go-Between-Us with a man coming east to tell others about Indian customs. When he got to Missouri he knew he would not be paid, so he went on his own path. He rode on iron horses. Sometimes he walked. He sold his necklaces for money to buy food. Then he fasted many days. In the land of Il-li-nois, a railroad man took him to Ohio. He then sold his silver sleeve holders, so he could again eat. Then his Indian clothing. He kept only his leggings and blanket. Other kind railroad men fed him and gave him free rides to this place. Near Altoona his moccasins wore out from walking and he sold his blanket for a pair of shoes. Everyone here says he is very brave. My brother said he is a fool.

July 9

Miss Monk said my dress won a prize at the fair in Philadelphia. The prize is money. Twenty whole dollars! Never have I had white people's money! What will I do with it?

Always, my grandmother told me that with every bit of good fortune comes some pain. Never did I understand this. Now I do. Belle Rain Water is so angry at me because I won the prize. I fear her anger. What can she do to me? I ask. But I know she can do something.

July 11

Today we had to pick our project for the summer. Because I won the dress prize Mrs. Camp Bell said I should let everyone pick before me from the list. I wanted Wapka to be my project. He needs help with his reading. But Belle Rain Water wanted him. Grandmother always told me that what we *should* do, not what we *wish* to do, is the true road. I let Belle Rain Water have Wapka. Perhaps he will teach her something.

I was left with Mary Beth, the little white girl who is a daughter of one of the teachers. She is ten winters and wants a playhouse. Her father, who teaches here, is too busy to make one. My project is to find something that can be made into a playhouse for her.

July 13

Heat sits on the land like a vulture. I keep the windows of our bedroom open at night. They have given us netting to put around our beds. I have moved my bed and Pretty Eagle's near the windows. I long to be out under the sky. Pretty Eagle is not eating well. I worry for her.

July 14

The boys and girls who are camping left for Tagg's Run. I almost asked to go along, but I cannot leave Pretty Eagle. She was so quiet, I thought she was going into a trance again. She does keep busy, though. She is learning to embroider. Her work is very pretty.

July 15

Today I went swimming with some other girls in the millrace. The water was so cool and nice. It reminded me of the rivers at home. We looked so silly in our bathe dresses. Miss Monk came along with us. When she left, Belle Rain Water took off her dress and bathed with no clothes on. "Take off your dress," she told me. I said no. "It is because you are a stick girl," she said. Then she laughed at me. "Stick girl will never be a woman."

I did not wish to break the rules. Pretty Eagle came later and enjoyed herself, too.

July 16

I find nothing to make a playhouse for Mary Beth. I was ready to fail in my summer project. Worse, little Mary Beth looks so sad. Then when weeding the flower garden I looked up and saw what can be made into a playhouse. It is an old outhouse. I asked Mr. Captain Pratt about it. He said to write a note to Mr. Bumpass and tell him what I need for to fix it. Here is my note:

Dear Mr. Bumpass:

Here is what we need:

First, clean out house. Second, whitewash. Third, new floor. Fourth, two new panes of glass. Fifth, lock and key to the door. Sixth, fence around house. Seventh, shelf on one side for dolls. Eighth, mend the holes in the roof.

Respectfully, Nannie Little Rose.

Also, please, little Mary Beth is very sad. Her father made the promise of a playhouse to her. With my people, a promise is sacred. Respectfully again.

July 17

My brother heard of my outhouse project and laughed. "Father wanted you to do an act of bravery," he said. "Wait until he finds out how you turned an outhouse into a playhouse. Or if I see him first, I will tell him for you." My brother makes small of me every chance he gets.

July 18

We had fresh lettuce and tomatoes from our gardens. The teachers call it salad. Our potato crop has turned out well. They are saying we will have twelve hundred bushels. Ten strong boys are helping the farm workers to pick them. Everyone is very proud.

July 19

Word comes that Spotted Tail and the other chiefs are coming at the end of the week on their way home from seeing our great father in Wash-ing-ton. Oh, I am so afraid! I hope what my brother tells me is not true! We must get ready for their visit. I am helping with the cooking again.

July 24

Old Grump Puss is working hard to fix the outhouse into a playhouse. I helped, but he does not talk to me. Only he grunts and gives orders. Mary Beth is so happy. It made my heart glad. But then I think, I hope my brother does not see my father before me and tell him this is my act of bravery.

July 25

The chiefs have returned. Another feast, but this time it was served outside on the tables under the trees. There were no words spoken about leaving. But then, after we had gone to bed, I woke to see someone standing over me. It was Red Road. She whispered that I should go into the hall with her.

"Do you want to go home?" she asked me. I said no.

"My brother Max wants to stay," she said. "So do most of the Sioux children. Except your brother. I will try to talk with my father and get him to let the Sioux children stay."

I could not sleep all night for worrying. But I am sure Red Road will have power with her father. He listens to what she has to say.

July 26

Pretty Eagle fainted again today. Everyone thinks it is from the heat. She is again in the infirmary. I stayed with her all afternoon. Then Spotted Tail came with Charles Tackett, Red Road's husband, to see her.

I stepped outside the room while they visited. "This place is not good for our children," I heard Spotted Tail say. "I must get money to take them home. The white captain says the government will not pay for them to go on the train. I have a friend in the town of Carlisle. I will ask him for money." Then they left.

Pretty Eagle awoke around fading-time. I asked her if she had a vision.

Only she smiled at me and said, "Your father will be proud of you. But more for what you will do in the white people's world than for any brave acts. You will make our people proud, don't worry, Little Rose."

But I do worry. Because my brave act is taking care of her.

July 27

It is so very hot! I do not blame Pretty Eagle for fainting. This afternoon we went swimming again and for a while I forgot my troubles. At supper everyone was talking about the Sioux children leaving. Word has traveled that Mr. Captain Pratt and Spotted Tail had angry words between them, that Mr. Captain Pratt told Spotted Tail he may take his own children home if he wishes, but not the other Sioux children. Is this true? I pray it is. I pray Red Road has been able to convince her father that the rest of us Sioux children should stay here.

Spotted Tail has gone to town to see his friend and get money.

July 28

Today two intolerable things happened. First Belle Rain Water bumped into me in the hall. "You are going home," she said. "This I heard and know to be true. Let us see what your fancy dress prize can do for you now."

The second thing was that my brother came to see me

when I was weeding the flower garden. He asked me for money.

I asked him what for.

He tells it that he is going home with Spotted Tail. He needs money for the train. Spotted Tail is getting money only for his own children, but will take my brother and Alford Two Leggings, if they have money.

Oh, my heart rose to hear this! But then I brought my ears back to my brother. I told him Mr. Captain Pratt won't let him go.

He puffs himself up then and says he would like to see Mr. Captain Pratt stop him.

I have no money, I say. He argues that I have the money from the dress prize, and if I don't give it to him, he will tell Spotted Tail that Pretty Eagle must be taken home because she faints all the time.

His words are like flint. They strike fear into my heart. I say Pretty Eagle does not faint all the time. Only he grins and says he knows she goes into trances. That he overheard our grandmother and Pretty Eagle talking about it one day.

I thought the sky would fall down on my head when he said that. But only he smiles at me.

Who have you told this to? I asked.

He says no one. Yet. But that if I don't give him money,

maybe so he will tell Spotted Tail. I gave him the money. What could I do?

July 29

Spotted Tail has returned from Carlisle and gathered forth his children for the trip home. It is true. He means to take only his children, Mr. Captain Pratt told him the government can't afford to send children here and not let them stay and learn.

We all knew Max and his three brothers did not wish to go, not even Paul. There was much screaming and crying. Red Road tried to calm her little brothers. Spotted Tail made them take off their citizens' clothing and put on their blanket clothing. He had to drag Max into the wagon.

Then he went in to Mr. Captain Pratt's office. In a short while I was called in. Spotted Tail wanted to take Pretty Eagle home! Oh, my heart beat like a drum.

"Nannie," Mr. Captain Pratt said to me. "He says she is too sickly to stay here. She does not wish to go. I have told him she is better off here, with our doctors and nurses. I told him you have made her your responsibility, that you have even given up going on an outing, to stay and care for her. Do you still wish to continue caring for her? That is the only way she can stay."

Spotted Tail looked at me. Mr. Captain Pratt looked at me. I said yes. I promised Mr. Captain Pratt and Chief Spotted Tail I could care for her. I also told them that the long trip home might be more bad for her than anything. Spotted Tail got very angry and tramped out.

I did not see my brother or Alford Two Leggings in the wagon. But I saw the canvas over the back of the wagon. And I think they were under it.

July 30

It has been discovered that my brother is gone. Also his friend, Alford. I am hiding my face from everyone. I think they can see on my face that I have helped my brother by giving him money. I am so ashamed.

July 31

Today came the thing I have dreaded. Mr. Captain Pratt sent for me. Could I lie to him about giving my brother the money? As I walked across the hot, dusty yard to his office, my head was spinning. I could not lie. That would dishonor my people. I did not have to tell him why I gave the money, but I had to tell him I gave it. This I knew. He would be angry. I would be punished.

Haye! Haye! Thanks be! He did not ask me. He just told me, with much sadness, that my brother and Alford Two Leggings have run away. "They will be caught and sent back," he promised.

Kanta-sa-wí, Plums-Red Moon
August 1

What spirit has come over me! All I can think of is home and the plains. My heart is sick for want of the tall grasses, the running streams, the sky that goes on forever, the mountains that are always there in the distance. I miss the sweet grass and sage, the sounds of my people. Is this because my brother has gone home and I stay here?

I miss the excitement of our Sun Dance, our celebration of new birth, new hope. For some who take part it is a way to say thank you to the Above Beings for special favors. It is part of our people.

August 2

The playhouse for Mary Beth is finished. She is so happy. She has all her dolls in there. It made me think of my part of the tipi at home and the chest I had made of buffalo hide and covered with paintings of our people. Red Road taught me how to do the paintings. In it I left my good dress and moccasins and blanket. They wait for me. But I sometimes think I will never see home again.

August 3

Every day I look out across the small wooden bridge and expect to see my brother and Alford Two Leggings returned to us. Why do I look for my brother? He took my money. He was always mean to me. Yet he will soon be home and I am here. He will ride his pony across the plains. He will be at the Sun Dance. Our people will praise him for what he has learned at school. Grandmother will make him his favorite foods. I wish I could talk with my grandmother. But I know what she would say. "Do not be like the hummingbird that tried to sit on the turkey eggs. Do not try to take on tasks for which you are not fit."

Tomorrow we are going on a trip to Dickinson College to hear about some of the white man's medicine called elec-tric-i-ty. I shall try not to think about my brother.

August 5

Too tired when we got home from Dickinson College yesterday to write. The lecture was very much fun. Professor Hines of the college had a little house on a table struck by some lightning, which he made from his elec-tric-i-ty. We all stood around the table and held hands. Two of the boys were shocked with the elec-tric-i-ty, and the rest of us felt it, too. But we were too busy laughing. The white man's medicine is very strong. The little house was destroyed.

August 6

The boys and girls who were camping at Tagg's Run came home. They are very hot and dirty and tired. All the teachers laughed when one boy said, "We are so glad to be home. We want to live in houses like civilized people." Does this mean that Indian children here will no longer want to live in tipis at home? Or swim in streams? Have we all lost our faces? Was my brother right for going home, before he loses his face? Oh, I am so confused.

August 7

I have a postal from Frances Bones. Here is what she wrote:

I am very busy and also very happy here. My work is not hard. I set the table, wash the dishes, make the beds, and help take care of a small girl of three winters. I have time for myself. But I think of you. Home seems like it never was. Will I ever be able to go back there? Are you swimming every day? How is Pretty Eagle? Yesterday I made ice cream and I have gone to a Quaker Meeting. It is like one of our councils. Everyone who wishes to, says words. Our paths will cross soon. Your friend, Frances Bones.

August 8

Pretty Eagle has had a postal from the agent at the Rosebud Agency. It said her father has taken another wife.

He has two now. I am so glad my father never took more than one after my mother would not let him wed Red Road. But this postal also said that one of Pretty Eagle's brothers is ailing. He pledged himself in the Sun Dance.

He fasted and allowed wooden skewers to be put through the skin around his shoulders. Then heavy buffalo skulls were hung by thongs from the skewers, and he dragged them around until their weight tore the skewers loose. All the while he was dancing around and praying: "*Wankan Tanka*, have mercy on me, let the tribe live long and bring back the buffalo. Let no one get sick so the tribe will increase."

Many young men do this every year. Some to pray for the tribe, some to give thanks for special favors. It means they will someday be great chiefs. But also some die. And some get sick. I hope Pretty Eagle's brother does not die. Many young braves have died from this. I am very worried.

August 9

They told us today that in a week we are going on a trip to Luray Caverns in Vir-gin-i-a. Our Uncle Samuel will not pay for the cost of the train trip. The big chiefs from the

Cumberland Valley and Shenandoah Valley railroads are allowing us to ride at no cost. All will go, Mr. Captain Pratt said. We will stay two nights at the Luray Inn. Everyone is very excited. But I am very worried. How can I leave Pretty Eagle? I have told this to Mrs. Camp Bell and Mr. Captain Pratt. Both have said I must go. "You have not been anywhere this summer, for worrying about Lucy, child," Mrs. Camp Bell said. "This is a real opportunity for you. The caverns are famous. And you will see the Cumberland Valley. It is like a gem. Come with us, Nannie. Miss Monk is not going, and she will keep a special eye out for Lucy. It is only for three days."

So I am going. Pretty Eagle herself said I should go and tell her about the caverns.

August 10

Miss Monk gave us money for our trip to Luray Caverns. She said it was from the sale of some of the pillowcases and sheets we made over the last months. Maybe so we bring home something pretty that strikes our eye. She said she will keep watch over Pretty Eagle, who is well and promises to stay out of the heat and eat and do her embroidery.

August 14

Pretty Eagle told me she is much worried for her brother. So tonight when all was quiet we sneaked outside and I did something I have not done since I am here. I burned the offerings of tobacco and red willow bark my grandmother gave me for when I am in need. I have kept them hidden in my room. Pretty Eagle and I prayed together that her brother should soon be well. "I wish we could do more," I told her.

"Maybe so we can," Pretty Eagle said. But she did not say what.

August 16

So much to do to make ready for our trip! The gardens must be weeded good. Our clothes must be washed and pressed. We girls will take parasols because the sun is so hot in Vir-gin-i-a. We had to learn how to use them. I worry about Pretty Eagle. She seems not to be eating. She said it is too hot and she is happy with small amounts of food and much water.

August 17

I have brought my diary and my pen and ink so I can write on my journey. I am writing by oil lamp in our room at Luray Inn. The other girls are all running in the halls. This morning we were up at the hour of four. It looked like night-middle-made. After breakfast I ran back upstairs to see if Pretty Eagle was awake, so I could say good-bye. In the hall Belle Rain Water stood in my path.

"She is not here," she said.

I asked, where is she?

Bells says she is having breakfast with Miss Monk in her room. I see a paper in Belle's hand. Did she leave me a note? I ask. I know that Pretty Eagle is so proud of learning to write, though she could not make the white man's words on paper as good as the rest of us.

Belle tells me the paper is a postal that she received yesterday.

For a moment I think I do not like the secret smile she is wearing. Then, before I can think on this matter, Belle grabbed my arm and says we are late. That we should be in the wagon. And they will not wait for us. She points out the window. Yes, the others are all in the wagons already, so we went down. But all day while we traveled on the cars, her secret smile hung in front of me.

August 18

My sleep brought bad medicine last night. I dreamed of Pretty Eagle. She had the skin of her shoulders pierced with skewers and was dragging around buffalo skulls in the Sun Dance. This dream is wrong. Women don't pledge themselves in the Sun Dance. I am very worried.

Today we went to the caverns. They were very beautiful. But I think the white people spoil much of the beauty with the elec-tric lights. We went up and down stairways and through passages. We saw great jagged forms. They called them sta-lag-mites. But there were so many forms and so many shadows that everyone saw something different.

"I see an angel's wing," Mrs. Camp Bell said. A Navajo boy cried out, "There is my blanket I lost years ago."

I saw Pretty Eagle with skewers in her shoulders, dragging buffalo skulls. But I told no one. Tomorrow we start the trip home. I am almost afraid to get there. Yet I know the train will not go fast enough.

August 19

Hot, so hot! Everyone has left the cars. I sit here and write. I must be careful not to get ink on my dress. The cars stopped near Antietam. Something is on the tracks and blocks our path. They must clear it. Mr. Captain Pratt took the boys to the nearby battlefield while we wait, to a part of it called Bloody Lane. Mrs. Camp Bell and some other teachers walked to town to get food and drink. I feel something clutching at my heart, like the claws of an eagle. I cannot rid myself of the feeling that this trip is bad medicine.

August 24

I have not written in this book for five suns. I could not, because my heart is on the ground. Pretty Eagle is dead!

Miss Monk told us when we came back. They were waiting for us, like chiefs about to have a council — Miss Monk and the little girls Pretty Eagle had for friends. Those little girls were crying when Miss Monk told me the words. And when she said them I sank down on Mother Earth, where my heart was. But Mother Earth was no longer there for me. I felt nothing beneath me. There was no place for me to go.

Miss Monk took me by the arm and tried to pick me up. I got up, but I started to run to the infirmary.

"She is not there," Miss Monk called after me. "She is buried in our cemetery."

I stopped and turned around to stare at them. They were looking at me, all of them, the teachers, the little girls who were Pretty Eagle's friends, and the students who had just come back from the trip with me. The little girls nodded in sadness. "We were there when they buried her," they said. And each in her own way told something of the ceremony.

I did not wait to hear. I ran again, toward the kitchen.

Woman-Who-Screams-A-Lot was in there working with some other girls. I ran right past them to where they keep the knives. I grabbed one up. Woman-Who-Screams-A-Lot tried to take it from me, but I slashed at the air near her and ran out the back door.

I cut my hair and slashed my clothing and arms. I was going to slash my face when Miss Monk and Mrs. Camp Bell and some of the children came running toward me. The teachers begged me to stop, but I would not.

Later they told me it was Belle Rain Water who grabbed

the knife and stopped me from slashing my face. They tell it that she is the only one who was strong enough. I wish I had slashed her with the knife, too.

August 26

Pretty Eagle is dead! She lies in the graveyard with Horace Watchful Fox, Dickens, and Elkannah. Old Grump Puss dug her grave and they buried her even as our train waited on the tracks outside Antietam! They did not even wait for me!

August 27

It comes to me in little pieces, like something broken. I heard things when I was in the infirmary, and I hear things now. I hear them whispering around me. Mr. Captain Pratt had asked Reverend Leverett from St. John's Church in Carlisle to be the chief man at the burial. And as chief man, the reverend could not wait for us to arrive on our train.

August 28

Oh, my pen cannot write the words! Pretty Eagle was in a trance when they buried her. Miss Monk told me this day that she had fainted and was in the infirmary only a day. When they went to see her she was not breathing. Oh, how can I write these words? Sometimes when she went into a trance Pretty Eagle looked as if she was not breathing! It was when she was in a deep trance, very far away, maybe so about to have a vision!

If this is so, then they buried her alive! And I was not here to protect her! I have failed in my one brave act. It was my duty to protect her, and I failed. Oh, I am worthless and so ashamed!

August 29

I tell myself I will no longer write in this book. What good are words? What have I to say that needs to be remembered? Only sadness. Yet, I must write. It is the only way I know who I am. Who I have become. So I will tell it.

I have prayed on it and gone over it again and again in my mind. I know Pretty Eagle was in a trance, because after they let me out of the infirmary, and before they made me move in with Mrs. Camp Bell, I was allowed to go to my room and get some things.

There I found a note from Pretty Eagle. It was under my pillow.

Here is what it said, in Pretty Eagle's poor last words:

My friend, if I trance still when you re-turn, do not get big with fear. I go make plea so my brother get well. He was much brave. I must be so, too. They will care for me here. Your dear friend always, Pretty Eagle.

Oh, if I were here! Oh, I could have stopped them!

Oh, Pretty Eagle, my friend. Did you wake from your trance and find yourself smothered with earth? And wonder where is your friend, Little Rose? I cannot think of it.

They make me sleep in the teachers' dormitory now with Mrs. Camp Bell. They think I will more harm myself. She took a scissor and, because my hair was much ragged, cut it the same all around. It is very short now. There are bandages all up and down my arms. Someone is with me at all times. They ask me five times a day if I am well. I am as well as someone can be who does not have a heart, I tell them. It is on the ground, and I do not wish to ever pick it up.

August 31

Last night I dreamed of my mouse spirit helper. He told me not to be sad, that Pretty Eagle had done what she was sent to do here. That they would remember her here for a long time. And she had schooled many little children not to forget their beginnings.

"But I failed in my one brave act," I told him.

"Do you think only of yourself, then?" he asked. "Pretty Eagle's time here was done. Instead of feeling sorry for yourself, think what else you could still do for her."

I woke still hearing his voice. I wish I could believe him. What can I do for Pretty Eagle?

I went to the infirmary, where I go each day to have my bandages changed. The nurse says I will have scars. Good. I will wear them and be proud, for Pretty Eagle.

Coming out of the infirmary I thought of what to do for Pretty Eagle. With my people we believe that when one dies her spirit stays at that place where she dies for many days. We also believe the spirit then has a long journey to make and should be provided with food. That's what my mouse spirit helper was trying to tell me.

So I went to the kitchen. By some good fortune no one was there. I took some food, some bread and some cheese, some meat and some fruit. I took it to Pretty Eagle's grave.

Oh, Pretty Eagle, I said, if I had only paid mind to Belle Rain Water's secret smile! That morning, when I went back upstairs to say farewell to you, the piece of paper she had in her hand was a message for me from Miss Monk. She wrote that she came to our room and found you sick and took you to the infirmary. Belle took the note and said she would give it to me.

Of course, she did not. She would not. She still hates me for winning the stupid dress prize, and so she kept from me that you were ill. Killing my mouse spirit helper was not enough. Because she kept the note from me, I left and you died.

I don't care what my mouse spirit helper says. What does he know? He's only a mouse. All he thinks of is food. Well, I've left the food for you on your journey. But I still say I have failed you so! My one act of bravery at this place was to care for you. And I have failed. How can I ever face my people?

Canwape-gi-wi, Tree-Leaves-Yellow Moon
September 2

I went again today to Pretty Eagle's grave. The food was gone! Haye! Haye! My mouse spirit helper was right. Pretty Eagle needed the food for her journey! I was so happy.

Then I met Old Grump Puss. "Did you leave food here?" he asked me.

I said yes.

"This is not a picnic ground. This is a cemetery. Have respect."

"I left it for my friend," I told him. "Her spirit needs it for her long journey."

"No more food!" He yelled the words at me. "Or I'll tell Captain Pratt. You Indians are all crazy."

But I have left more food. How can Pretty Eagle find her way on the long journey she must now make if she is hungry?

With my people, when a chief or important brave dies, they bury him on a wood platform high in the trees. His horse or dog are slain and placed near him at the burial place to guide him on his journey. A Spirit Keeper is chosen to mourn for a year. I would become a Spirit Keeper for

Pretty Eagle. But they would not let me do that here. So I will give away some of her things in her name.

My arms still hurt. Soon the bandages come off. I have told Mrs. Camp Bell I want to go back to my own room. "I will harm myself no longer," I said. She said she must ask Mr. Captain Pratt.

September 4

Today I was summoned to Mr. Captain Pratt's office. Miss Monk and Mrs. Camp Bell were there. Mr. Captain Pratt said how sorry he was about Lucy. I did not tell that she was in a trance. That is my burden to carry alone, forever.

"Do I have your promise that you will harm yourself no more?" he asked.

"Once done, cutting the hair and slashing the arms at the death of a loved one is not done again," I said.

Miss Monk then said how sorry she was. I told her it is my fault about Pretty Eagle, not hers.

"We can't have you thinking this," Mrs. Camp Bell said.

I told her then that it was my one act of bravery, to care for Pretty Eagle. That I had done no great act of bravery since I was here, to make my people proud. That my heart was on the ground. And I would make no move to pick it up.

"Large acts of bravery are good," Mrs. Camp Bell said, "but in the white people's world there is not much chance to do them. So we try to do small acts of kindness. They are just as important. You have done many of them since you are here, Nannie. You made the suit for Albert Talks With Bears. You made the playhouse for Mary Beth. You took Lucy into your room. Your people should be very proud."

I looked at her. "This is true?" I asked.

"Acts of bravery make us proud," she said. "Acts of kindness make us beautiful. So pick your heart up off the ground. You have done well."

I promised I would think on her words.

September 6

The food is gone from Pretty Eagle's grave again. Did her spirit take it? Or did Old Grump Puss? I did not see him, so I do not know. Students have returned from their outings. School starts soon. There is a taste in the air of *ptanyetu*, changeable-time, the white people's autumn. At home my people will be hunting whatever they find on the reservation for the lean days of *waniyetu*, snow-exists-time, winter. If any meat is brought in, it will be cut by the women and hung to dry in the sun, then put into folded rawhide and stored away in the ground.

Then my people will wait for the white people's gift of cattle. The young braves will "hunt" them, shoot them down, and then they will be butchered. But it is not the same as the buffalo hunt in The-Time-That-Was-Before. This my father told me.

Here I sew a warm dress. I am back in my room. The bandages are off my arms. The scars are very bright red. I think of Pretty Eagle every time I see them.

They have taken her bed from our room. But I still see it and her there every time my eyes turn in that direction. And she still hovers over me, like something heavy on my heart.

There is one task I must do. It is right in the middle of my path. And I have been walking around it every day. It is time now to speak to Belle Rain Water.

I have passed her in the hall. I have worked across from her in the kitchen. I feel her eyes on me when I am not looking. I must make things right. But I am confused.

She held back the note Miss Monk wrote to me. Yet she stopped me from slashing my face. Is there some good spirit in her that I have not seen? Do I wish to see it? If I see it, will I lose my anger at her for causing Pretty Eagle's death? I must not do that. I must hold on to my anger and take my revenge. I must pray and fast so I can know how to do this thing.

September 7

The boys and girls who have come back from outings are happy and content. They have made money, and Mr. Captain Pratt has put their money in the white people's banks. They will be given it when they return home. It is good to have Frances Bones back. We have spoken in soft words about Pretty Eagle. We all miss her.

September 10

I have been leaving food every day for Pretty Eagle at the grave. And every day it is gone. Is Pretty Eagle's spirit taking it? Or someone else? I must be sure, so I keep leaving food. Maybe so it is Belle Rain Water.

We were told today that Mr. Captain Pratt sent a postal to Doekitshis, Pretty Eagle's father, right after she died. This day a postal has come from Doekitshis. He wrote back that Pretty Eagle had died the year before and come back to life again.

At dinner, all the teachers were puzzled over the meaning of the words. But the girls at our table said nothing. We know the words either mean that the fainting was the first part of death. Or that Pretty Eagle went into trances. I saw Belle Rain Water looking at me at the table. I did not look back. When we left the dining room, she came to me. Her face was very white.

"We must light the council fire," she said.

I just stared at her. I knew we must meet sooner or later, but I was not ready for it so soon. Yes, I answered, but when?

She said when the others go to the evening discussion group I was to meet her outside our rooms. In the little alcove at the end of the hallway.

I did not eat at dinner. I took only some tea. I have been trying to fast, and praying to our spirits and to the white people's god. I wish my mouse spirit helper would speak to me, but he has not done so. Perhaps I am not worthy. I took a very hot bath. It is not the sweat bath of home, but it purified my body for the meeting with Belle Rain Water. She comes now. I shall meet her.

September 11

Last night I met with Belle Rain Water. At first I thought I must be ready to fight her if she wished it, though she is much larger than me. In her hand was a willow stick on which were fastened the yellow feathers of a bird. And that of an eagle. I thought she meant to hit me with it. But I stood firm.

She told me it was a Hopi prayer stick, then she held it out to me. I did not take it. She explained that it is for a very young person who has died. She said it was for Pretty Eagle. And if I placed it in the sun in my room, when the sun journeyed across the sky each day he would see it and carry each prayer away.

I told her I would not take it. That she was not worthy to speak Pretty Eagle's name. That she helped kill her when she kept Miss Monk's note from me. "You knew Pretty Eagle was sick and needed me," I said.

Then she looked ashamed and said she did not know Pretty Eagle had trances. That from the letter read at supper she now knew. "She was buried alive," she said.

For a moment I could not speak of the matter. Then she said she did not mean to hurt Pretty Eagle, that she kept the note from me to hurt me. That she thought I was her enemy. She thought I was a witch.

I asked her what did I ever do to make her think I was a witch? I have never hurt you, I told her. And you were mean to me since I came here.

She said she was jealous of me, that my face was so pretty, that hers was not since she had the spotted sickness. She said I was like a willow tree, and she was like a giant oak. And I was always doing things better than her and getting praise. She was jealous.

Was this any reason to help kill Pretty Eagle? I asked again. And again she said she did not think Pretty Eagle would die, she thought she had fainted as she did before.

"Even if you only thought it was fainting," I told her, "it was a mean trick. And now you are stealing the food from her grave." "What food?" she asks. So I told her how I leave food every day so Pretty Eagle's spirit has nourishment for its long journey. And somebody is taking it. "At first I thought it was Old Grump Puss," I said. "Now I think it's you."

"I would not do this thing," she said.

But I do not believe her. And the first chance I get I will lie in wait and see. She was pleading with me, now, for forgiveness. But I could not forgive her. "Keep your prayer stick," I said. "I cannot accept it. Use it yourself. I cannot dishonor Pretty Eagle's memory."

September 12

I feel so much better now that I faced Belle Rain Water. I feel as if I have done something for Pretty Eagle. Today I caught Belle looking at me in cooking again. Often I feel her eyes on me. But she says nothing. I think she is suffering. Good.

Students who went home to reservations are back. A Cheyenne boy says all the little children on his reservation seem different. A Chippewa girl said she missed her bed and washing room.

When Pretty Eagle first came they did not go through her things for fear she would have a spell. I have given Pretty Eagle's comb to Frances Bones, her flute, made from an eagle's wing bone, to Almeda Heavy Hair. The otter fur with which she wrapped her braid when she first came to

Carlisle to Maggie Stands Looking, and her awl case to Ada Fox Catcher.

September 15

We are in school again. I still grieve for Pretty Eagle. I miss Red Road. I know if she were here she would have good words to say to me. I have been thinking of her so much this day. She weighs on my heart and my mind. Is she all right? I have thought of her so that for a whole day I did not think of Pretty Eagle, and even forgot to leave the food on her grave.

September 16

Haye! Haye! A postal from Red Road. Now I know why I thought of her so yesterday. Last week she had her baby. Her letter says that when she told me of the child last June she was already five moons into having it. "My loose dresses kept my secret," she wrote. "And being it is my first, it was an easy secret to keep. Now the baby is born, a month early. But he is well. A boy! We have named him Peter Spotted Deer. There is much rejoicing and my husband and I will be able to make the trip back to Carlisle by November."

I am much happy for Red Road, and that she is coming back. There is more news in the postal. Red Road writes that my brother had come back to the reservation and stayed two days and left. This was even before she had her baby. She writes that she thinks he is on his way back to us and my father asks if maybe so Mr. Captain Pratt will let him know if my brother returns to Carlisle. I ran to see Mr. Captain Pratt. He says if my brother returns, there will be a place for him here if he promises to behave himself. My heart is lighter. But I worry about my brother, traveling alone.

September 17

Today when I went to Pretty Eagle's grave Old Grump Puss was there, waiting for me. "I thought I told you to stop leaving food," he said. "I came here yesterday and the day before and there was food on the grave."

I told him I had not left it. I told him for two days I had forgotten to leave it. "You lie," he said. "And I shall report this to Captain Pratt."

I did not leave the food. Who could have brought it? Is someone playing a trick on me?

September 18

I am here almost one year. The dark comes sooner now. We wear our warmer clothing. The leaves have begun to fall on Pretty Eagle's grave.

Today, in cooking class, Woman-Who-Screams-A-Lot scolded. "Someone has been taking food to the cemetery. This is desecration. Of the graves and food." Then she looked at me. "You are to go to the office of Captain Pratt. Now."

So I left. As I walked across the cold yard, I knew I was in trouble. And I was.

Mr. Captain Pratt was most upset with me. "You must not take food to the cemetery," he said. "Mr. Bumpass tries to keep the graves neat. Food brings rats and raccoons and other vermin."

I told him about Pretty Eagle's spirit needing the food for its journey. That her spirit might never leave this place if it did not have nourishment.

He was about to scold more when the door opened and Belle Rain Water walked in. "I have been leaving food at the grave, too," she said. "For Pretty Eagle's spirit."

She looked at me with defiance in her eyes as she said it, as if to say, I will take any path I can to make you forgive me for what happened to Pretty Eagle. But it did not work. I still do not forgive her. Even though she shared my punishment. Mr. Captain Pratt said we were both to accept whatever punishment Miss Cafrey, our cooking teacher, thought best. She says we must both stay after class and scour pots for the rest of the week. All the time we scoured today I felt Belle Rain Water watching me. As if to say, See, you would be doing this all by yourself if not for me. All the time, I did not speak to her.

September 24

I have not written for five days because I am still staying after cooking class and scouring pots. My hands are red and raw. And still I do not speak to Belle Rain Water, even though she takes the biggest pots and does them. She is very quick and strong.

All the time I think of my brother. There is no word yet from him. Is he out of money? Must he sell his blanket Indian things to get food, like Wapka? My brother does not have Wapka's bravery. He cannot go without his meat. Soon it will be *Canwape-kasna-wi*, Tree-Leaves-Shaken-Off Moon, October. Even scouring pots in the kitchen I am warm and my stomach is full. And I wonder if my brother is in some cold corner of the earth someplace, hungry and half naked.

Today when we finished the pots and I took off my wet apron, Belle Rain Water came over to me. "You have not left food for Pretty Eagle for days," she said.

I had to answer. She stood close. "What do you care?" I asked. She said she cared because she left food, too. She then asked me if I thought she would admit to it if she hadn't. I told her I never thought about her at all. She paid no mind to that, just went right on talking about how she left the food so Pretty Eagle could go on her journey.

Then she said Pretty Eagle's spirit was still at the cemetery, that she could feel it there. I had felt it, also. But this was just her way of spreading her blanket near me. I would not allow her to. I still must honor Pretty Eagle's memory, and not forgive her enemy.

Only Belle smiled. "With my people, life has no beginning and no end," she said. Then she told how, with her people, the dead add their strength and counsel to the living. And she left food because Pretty Eagle has a journey to make, and she wanted to make up for the bad thing she had done.

Again I told her she could not make up for it. But she said she could try. Then she smiles and tells me how stubborn I am, and asks if all Sioux are so stubborn. But I do not answer. Still she goes on talking. She has more words in her, this girl, than she knows what to do with. She tells me she knows a way that Old Grump Puss won't know if we leave food tonight. "Do you want to know what I know?" she asks.

I just stared at her.

She turned and took up a dish. On it she put some bread and meat, which she took from the larder. Also some cheese and an apple. "I will leave the food," she said. "You can come with me or stay and mope." And she started to walk out.

"Old Grump Puss will find it!" I yelled after her.

At the door she turned and said that Old Grump Puss

has a week off. And this was one chance for Pretty Eagle to get the food for her journey. "Will you take a plate and come, too?" she asked. "Or will you let her eat your stubbornness?"

I took up a plate and followed her. It was starting to rain and coming on to fading-time outside. We walked in the rain to the cemetery and left the food. We did not talk. But as we set it down Belle Rain Water said a prayer in her language. I said one in my own.

September 25

Today it rained very hard. Cold and dreary. But at breakfast Belle Rain Water came into the dining room very late and very wet. A teacher scolded her. "Where have you been? You will be sick! Go get on dry things."

On her way she stopped by our table and looked down at me. "The food is gone," she said. She was smiling.

I just looked down at my own food and ate and said nothing. But inside me I felt warm. Was it possible? Did Pretty Eagle take the food? Is she on the way to her long journey? If so, I have Belle Rain Water to thank. But how can I thank her when she helped kill Pretty Eagle?

September 26

I have been to the cemetery in the rain. The food was gone. I did not feel Pretty Eagle's spirit. Is she gone? Will she return after she completes her long journey? Will her spirit come back to guide us here? Sometimes they do. To stop my confusion about Pretty Eagle and Belle, and my worry about my brother, I have offered to head the committee to raise money for the starving Russians this winter. I did not know that other tribes in other lands were starving, too. My goal is sixty dollars.

September 27

Last night I dreamed of my mouse spirit helper. He told me I should forgive Belle Rain Water. "She did not know what would happen with Pretty Eagle," he said. "She did not know of the trances. You must forgive her. Sometimes it is more honorable to forgive your enemy than to stay angry. Pretty Eagle has accepted the food you and Belle left. Pretty Eagle says she wishes you to do this in her name."

I woke in night-middle-made, thinking, How can I? When is it more honorable to forgive your enemy than to stay angry? I would have to have a good reason, and I had none. Oh, if only I had a sign. If only Pretty Eagle would give me one. Then I went to sleep again. And again my mouse spirit helper came to me with more words.

"Your brother will be here soon," he said. "You must always be listening and watching for him. And be ready to help, for he will need you."

Now I have two messages from my spirit helper. Like Belle Rain Water, he seems to have more words than he knows what to do with. How could I help my brother? I do not know where he is. There has been no word from him. What am I to do?

We have a new piano. A friend of Mrs. Camp Bell gave it. I am going to learn to play. We were told today that in the last eleven moons the boys in our shops made 13 wagons, 1 buggy, 177 sets of double harnesses, 6,744 pieces of tinware, and 160 pairs of shoes. Also they have mended many pairs of boots and done much work outside the school to repair roofs. The blacksmith shop fixed farm tools for nearby farmers. Most of the clothing for our 180 boys has been done in the tailor shop.

Also in the sewing room we girls make our own garments and underwear, sheets and pillowcases. Tomorrow I am going to learn to make fudge.

September 28

Today it was raining hard outside. Rain poured down as if the world would float away, the way it must have been in the time of the chief Noah that the white preacher talks about. No one ventured outside. I was stirring my fudge in the pot on the stove when Mr. Captain Pratt came in. He was wearing oilskins and dripped water. Woman-Who-Screams-A-Lot quickly fetched him hot tea to drink and he came and watched what we girls were cooking. All the time he is saying we do so well, that the stew for supper will be welcome because of the rain.

Before he leaves he is talking to Woman-Who-Screams-A-Lot. I listen because I am nearby. I hear him say he has word from the stationmaster in town. A blanket Indian has been seen hiding under the eaves of the station all last night in the rain. Who can it be? Woman-Who-Screams-A-Lot asks. He says he does not know, but Mr. Bumpass has the week off and he can't ask any of the teachers to go and find out. Not in this weather. The blanket Indian will just have to wait until it stops.

I continue to stir my fudge. And with each stir the thought grows inside me. Is this my brother, come all the way across the country to be left alone now, and cold in the rain? Is this what my mouse helper was trying to tell me?

But what could I do? Mr. Captain Pratt would never let me go alone in a wagon. I could not guide the horse on the muddy roads. And even if I could, how could I tell Mr. Captain Pratt it is my brother when I am not sure? Oh, mouse spirit helper, help me, I prayed.

I was thinking so hard, my fudge almost boiled over and made a mess on the stove. Belle Rain Water came over just in time and grabbed the pot handle and moved it off the heat.

Then something happened. She stood very close to me. Her eyes looked into mine, but they were not her eyes, but Pretty Eagle's eyes! And inside me I heard Pretty Eagle's voice:

"Go ask Mr. Captain Pratt to let you fetch your brother," the voice said.

I stumbled past Belle Rain Water and went to the door, where our oilskins hung on pegs. "Where do you think you are going?" Woman-Who-Screams-A-Lot yelled. But I did not answer. I ran across the yard to Mr. Captain Pratt's office, slipping in the mud all the way.

Mr. Captain Pratt shook his head when I told what I

wanted. "You want to drive a wagon to town, Nannie?" he asked. "How do you know this is your brother?"

I told him I knew in my heart that it was. And we could not leave him there. "He will be hungry and cold and sick," I said. "He will die of pneumonia, like Elkannah and the others."

Only he shakes his head again and says he cannot let me go alone. If I had an older person to go with me, perhaps he would permit it, he says. Someone strong, to manage the horse. But all the teachers are busy and he can't ask them to go out in this weather anyway.

But I am still filled with the sound of Pretty Eagle's words in my head. And the way I saw her eyes instead of Belle Rain Water's. And it was then that I knew what I must do.

If Pretty Eagle could come to me through the eyes of Belle Rain Water, then wasn't she trying to tell me more than to go get my brother? Wasn't she trying to tell me that I should forgive Belle?

To do this, I knew I must humble myself. I must eat my pride and go to my enemy and ask her help. To save my brother who was weary from travel and sick and cold, maybe so.

"If I get someone older who is willing to come, can I go?" I asked Mr. Captain Pratt.

He asks what if I get sick? I told him I am healthy. And so is the girl I will ask to go with me. So he gives permission then, and I run back to the kitchen and ask Belle Rain Water if she will go to town with me and fetch my brother, who is at the station.

She does not ask how I know it is my brother. Only she smiles and says, let's go.

Belle got the strongest horse from the barn and hitched him up. We both wore oilskins. I brought food for my brother. And blankets. It was not far to town, but the rain and mud made it seem farther. Belle held the horse strong so he wouldn't slip in the rain. Not once did she ask how I knew this blanket Indian was my brother. But what if it isn't? I thought. Will she think I am a fool? But I could not worry about that. Because I trusted my mouse spirit helper. And Pretty Eagle, who had come to me through Belle's eyes.

When we got there the station seemed empty. We went inside to where the stationmaster sat. And he took us to my brother, who was in a small back room, wet and shivering.

"Haye!" I said. "You are back."

He was dirty. He smelled. He was dripping water on the floor. He looked half blanket Indian and half whipped dog. "I am back," Whiteshield said to me.

I told him how happy I was to see him alive. I told him we thought he was dead. And then we just stared at each other, not knowing what to say. I could see my brother's eyes walking away from me. Ashamed for how he had treated me. Ashamed for running away. Belle Rain Water spoke then, telling him to change into the dry clothing we had brought. She thrust the clothes at him.

My brother clutched the clothing. "They will take me back?" he asked.

I told him what Mr. Captain Pratt had said. Then I asked what had happened to Alford Two Leggings. Whiteshield said he went back to his people. I asked why he did not stay with our people.

Then Belle says to let him change and have some food, and he can tell us on the way back in the wagon. She was right, of course. And my brother did tell us.

Our grandfather is dying, he said. But he wanted Whiteshield to return to school.

I felt a large pain in my heart. I asked him if he came back for Grandfather. He said no. He said our father has taken a second wife and she does not want him around. She said Whiteshield is boastful. And to please her, our father gave Whiteshield's pony to her father when he asked to marry her.

A second wife! I gasped. Then I asked, Who is she?

She is Stands Firm. She is not pretty. I remember how she always went against the Sioux teaching about the loud woman not being approved. Why did my father marry her?

"She no longer lets him wear his chief's clothes," my brother said.

I asked how my mother permitted this marriage. Whiteshield told us that our mother had no say. I know I should feel glad that my father did not let my mother rule him in this decision. Still, I do not like this woman. She is bad medicine.

Whiteshield said she is mean to our mother. Oh, why didn't my father take Red Road for his second wife? She would not be mean. She has a beautiful baby now and would have done much to make our tipi a happy place.

But it was not only for this that he left, Whiteshield told us. On the reservation, he spoke like a gentleman. He thought because he can read and write and cipher, he could help them. Couldn't he name all the states in the Union and sing a dozen Christian hymns? Nobody cared. Also, he said, at home there are no wagons to be mended, no horses to be shod, no shoes to fix. There was no place for him. So he came back to us.

My brother is very thin. I asked him how he got here. He looked shy and asked my forgiveness. He took my good deerskin dress with the pony beadwork and sold it to white people. The same with my moccasins and blanket. Red Road and her husband gave him some money and he started the trip with Tackett, who was going on a trading journey. He went as far as Yankton with Whiteshield, then got him on a train. When my brother's money ran out he worked and begged and starved and gave away his own things.

Then he asked if I was angry because he sold my things.

"No," I said. "I am glad you are here with me."

"I will not shame you anymore," he said. "Or Mr. Captain Pratt. There is no other place for me. Warriors are from The-Time-That-Was-Before. I will work hard, you will see."

Canwape-kasna-wi, Tree-Leaves-Shaken-Off Moon
October 15

More blanket Indian children have arrived. Am I becoming white by talking about them that way? They are not Sioux, but Arapaho, Cheyenne, and Comanche. They look a hundred miles lost, and very sad. We have done our best to welcome them and all are very busy.

Now the weather has turned warm and fine. Most days the sky is very blue. The leaves of the trees are all colors. The white people call it Indian summer, but I do not know why. It has nothing to do with us. The white people still seem very strange to me sometimes, but I am feeling more and more at home here.

Although my heart drops on the ground every day when I think of Pretty Eagle, every day I bend down and pick it up. And I think her spirit has returned from its long journey, for when I go to visit her grave, sometimes I think she is still here. I feel her in the warm October sun. I hear her voice in the rustle of the leaves on the ground. I think she will always be here, maybe so.

I have forgiven Belle Rain Water. My mouse spirit helper was right. Sometimes it is more honorable to forgive our enemies than to hate them. But I have not dishonored the memory of Pretty Eagle because if not for Belle Rain Water taking me to town that day to fetch my brother, he would have been very ill and died. The doctor said this. I am so glad I listened to my spirit helper.

For two weeks after my brother came back, he was in the infirmary, very sick. This is why I have not written in my diary in two weeks. I have been caring for my brother as well as doing my chores and schoolwork. Belle Rain Water has been caring for him also.

Belle has made up, in part, for what she did with Pretty Eagle. Now we work together in the kitchen and often we go to Pretty Eagle's grave to leave fall flowers.

Also I cannot forget it was Belle who stopped me from slashing my face. I asked her why. "Your face is so pretty," she said again. "I could not let you scar it. Like mine is scarred."

"Your face is beautiful now," I told her.

And this is true. I have given much thought to Mrs. Camp Bell's words about acts of kindness making us beautiful. The words must be true, because Belle has done many acts of kindness for me and I no longer think of her as ugly. I have even accepted the prayer stick from her and placed it in the sun in my room. And every day, when the sun journeys across the sky, he sees the prayer stick and carries my prayers away with him. For my grandfather and grandmother, for my people.

October 16

I have received a postal from Red Road. My grandfather has died. I mourn for him. I light the sacred tobacco from the pouches my grandmother gave me and pray with the prayer stick. My grandmother is still well, though, and sends me words that are good medicine. I write back and tell her I will return home in the spring.

October 18

Belle says that when spring comes we will put violets on Pretty Eagle's grave again. My brother is better and has settled in. He studies and works hard.

Red Road writes that she and her husband have started east with the baby and will be here by Thanksgiving. Haye! Haye! I cannot wait to see the baby!

Mr. Captain Pratt has been having private talks with every student in our class. He is making sure we are doing the right lessons for what we want to become.

I told him I wish to be a teacher and help other blanket Indian children to learn. He said my work is so good that I will be able to go on to Higher Education. This means I will go to a white people's college. He gave me some names. One of them is Bloomsburg. Mr. Captain Pratt said he will make a good word for me with people he knows there.

He also said that by the time I finish Higher Education there will be schools on my reservation, and I can go back there and teach if I wish.

Oh, how proud I would be to do this!

Then he asked if I would be the pilgrim woman in the play for Thanksgiving. It is the chief role. "I am much frightened," I told him. "I would rather touch a live enemy with a lance."

"Do you have a lance, Nannie Little Rose?" he asked.

I said no.

"Do you have any enemies here?"

I said no to that, too. For it is so.

"Then perhaps you can touch the other children with this performance. For you are most suited to be a pilgrim.

You have overcome much in your first year here, more than many others."

So I said yes. Red Road will be here then and she will see me as the pilgrim woman. Yes, I am frightened, but I suppose it is an act of kindness to do this for Mr. Captain Pratt. Then I also think, because I am so frightened, it is an act of bravery, too. Maybe so.

Epilogue

After she completed her education at Carlisle, Nannie Little Rose went home to the Rosebud Agency. By then, her beloved grandmother was ailing, her father had taken a third wife, and the Sioux Indians were existing on annuities — periodic issuing of food and fabric — given in payment for lands taken by the government.

Seeing the abject poverty and despair, Nannie Little Rose returned to Carlisle to board while she attended the preparatory school of Bloomsburg. After graduating from Bloomsburg in 1889, she returned again to the Dakotas as a schoolteacher at the Day School for Sioux children at the Pine Ridge Agency. Her grandmother had now died. Her brother, Charles Whiteshield, finished Carlisle and returned to the Rosebud Agency, where he joined the police force.

December of 1890 was important to Nannie Little Rose and her brother. Charles, with other mounted Indian police, was sent to arrest Sioux Chief Sitting Bull before he set out to join Sioux Ghost Dancers who were viewed by authorities as becoming wild and threatening. In the confusion, Sitting Bull was shot.

The authorities saw the Ghost Dance melee as the beginnings of an uprising. The military was called in. The Sioux were about to surrender when someone fired a gun, and in what has become known as the massacre at Wounded Knee, over 145 Indian men, women, and children were slaughtered.

Charles Whiteshield left the police, joined Buffalo Bill's Wild West Show, and traveled the world with the show, performing as a Sioux Indian chief. He never married, and died in 1922.

While helping care for the survivors of Wounded Knee, Nannie Little Rose met a young doctor named Henry Yellow Hair Cadman, a mixed-blood Sioux who was educated in the white-run Indian schools. They married in 1891 and had four sons.

Nannie's firstborn, Chauncy Eagle-Horn, lied about his age, volunteered for the army at sixteen, and was killed in France in World War I. A grandson served with the Air Force in World War II, and a great-grandson was a Sioux demonstrator in 1969 when Indians occupied Alcatraz Island in San Francisco Bay to reclaim it as Indian land,

and offered to buy it for $24 in beads and cloth, the amount the whites had paid for Manhattan Island.

Nannie Little Rose and her husband served the Plains Indians for years and retired to Oklahoma, where he treated Indian children and she was active in the Red Cross and in lobbying for Indian rights. She stayed in touch with Mrs. Campbell, her teacher at Carlisle, until the woman died in 1930.

She always kept the prayer stick given to her by Belle Rain Water and corresponded with Belle, who became a nurse, married, and had five children. Nannie Little Rose died in 1952 at eighty-five, the grandmother of five and great-grandmother of six. She left her diary to Lucy Rose, a baby great-granddaughter.

A constant supply of violets was kept on Lucy Pretty Eagle's grave until 1983. To this day, nobody knows who left them.

Life in America
in 1880

Historical Note

By 1880 the United States government had all but defeated America's Indians. The buffalo were gone, thanks to Western army officers who encouraged the killing of them to deny the Indians their most basic resource. And with the buffalo went the hunting tradition of the Plains.

Having, for the most part, confined the Indians to reservations, the government, in cooperation with various missionary and church groups, decided to educate the Indians. But education could not be accomplished without taking away their identity. It was decided that the Indians must be made to change their appearance and forget their language, religion, and customs.

This goal was to be accomplished at Indian schools. And in this era many sprung up across the country.

The most famous was the Carlisle Indian Industrial School, in Carlisle, Pennsylvania, which was started in 1879 by Captain Richard Henry Pratt, who had served in the Union Army in the Tenth Cavalry in the Civil War. After the war, when he was posted at Fort Arbuckle in

Indian Territory on the frontier, Pratt came to know the Indians, and decided that they could be assimilated into white society if they were educated and taught white ways. His first experiment was at Fort Marion in Saint Augustine, Florida, where he had taken some Indian prisoners. He saw that they were taught to read and write English and found them employment. Feeling successful in this venture, he approached the government to open a school in the East for the education of American Indians.

Carlisle Barracks in Pennsylvania had been an army post since the French and Indian War (1754–63). During the American Revolution the Continental Army used it as the first artillery school and arsenal. In 1794 it was a center for state militia during the Whiskey Rebellion. And in 1807 it became the U.S. Army's first cavalry school.

During the Civil War, Confederates burned the post and afterward it was rebuilt as a cavalry school for the army. Today it is the U.S. Army War College, but when Pratt set his heart on it, it had been abandoned for several years.

In 1879 Pratt acquired Carlisle Barracks for his school and made his trip that October to the Rosebud and Pine Ridge Sioux agencies in the Dakota Territory to seek Indian children.

The first Lakota Sioux children were brought to Carlisle

that fall, three years after General George Custer and 215 American soldiers were killed by Cheyenne and Oglala Sioux Indians. Geronimo and his Apaches would not surrender their way of life for another several years. Those first Sioux children who came to Carlisle could not have been happy there. But it was their only chance for a future.

Immediately upon arriving, their "Indianness" was taken from them. Hair was cut, and blankets, moccasins, leggings, deerskin dresses, and jewelry were all taken. The boys were put in military uniforms, the girls in Victorian-style dresses. Shoes went on their feet. And not only were they forbidden to speak their own language, but here they met children of other Indian tribes, who spoke different languages. Fortunately the Plains Indians had a kind of sign language by which they could communicate with one another. And this they put into immediate use.

A few Sioux children may have picked up some words of English from traders on the reservation, but they were the exceptions. Most of the Sioux children could not speak a word of English, and for that reason Captain Pratt had not wanted them. He preferred the Cheyenne, Arapahoe, Kiowa, Comanche, and other Indian tribes of the Plains who already had reservation schools. But the federal government said he must go to Spotted Tail's and Red Cloud's reservations because "the children would be hostages for the good behavior of their people."

The ages of the children at Carlisle were between the early teens and the middle twenties. And it was really a vocational school, with the purpose of teaching the children to make their way in the world in the trades — as farmers, homemakers, or in industry — after they learned the basics of reading, writing, history, geography, sewing, cooking, and Christianity. Sometimes it took as long as a year for them to learn to give voice to themselves in even broken English.

Everyone did manual labor. Girls and boys gardened. Girls washed and sewed clothing. Boys carried wood, plowed fields, and worked in the shops making tinware and mending harnesses and shoes.

Every moment was accounted for. There were religious classes, band practice, baseball, football, debating teams, school plays, singing practice — everything that was offered in regular schools. And, as in regular schools, some Indian children took to the lessons and enjoyed them and did well, and others resisted, made trouble, fought with teachers, stole things, and ran away.

In the summer some children went home to visit their reservations, and some went on "outings," a system set up by Captain Pratt in which they worked with local farmers or Quaker families for pay and learned how to act in the outside world. This was part of Pratt's plan to "de-Indianize" them, by forcing them to live in another culture.

There were also field trips to Luray Caverns in Virginia, to Philadelphia, to Mount Alto, to the circus, to Dickinson College, or to Mount Holly Paper Mill. There was even, in later years at the school, a newspaper — *Eadle keatah toh*, or *The Morning Star*, which, while it carried school news, was also concerned with Indian issues in general. And it was used by Captain Pratt as a private platform from which to spread his ideas about teaching.

There was much sickness at Carlisle in those first years, and many students died. It was said that Indians were susceptible to tuberculosis. But surely the abrupt "sea change" they underwent, going from reservations to the white-run school, where they were forced to forget their past, were put under stress to learn, and were mixed with so many strangers, contributed to the spread of disease. Although Pratt supplied proper food and sanitary facilities, and had a small hospital with a nurse and doctor on hand, the students still got sick and died from tuberculosis, measles, and scrofula, among other things.

The small but impressive cemetery one can visit today

on the Carlisle grounds attests to.that. There are the names on the gravestones, simply but impressively engraved — *Martha Anton, Pawnee; Percy Whitebear, Cheyenne; Herbert J. Littlehawk, Sioux; Raleigh James, Washoe; Albert Jackson, Seneca; Dickens, Arapahoe; Dora Morning, Cheyenne.*

And then there is *Lucy Pretty Eagle*, who died only four months after her arrival. There is conflicting data about when she arrived. Some say 1883. Others say 1893. And the date on her headstone is questioned also. The cause of her death is unknown, but her father had written to Captain Pratt that he was concerned about her health. "She died the year before but come back to life again," her father wrote. This "dying" could have been fainting, because Indians referred to fainting or epileptic siezures as dying. And the Sioux very much believed in ghosts.

Some research indicates that Lucy may not have been dead when she was buried. She could have been in a self-induced trace, to try to appeal to spiritual powers for any number of reasons.

By now, Lucy's name at Carlisle has been integrated into folklore. There are those who have gone on record as saying that the building in which Lucy stayed at Carlisle — now known as Coren Apartments — is haunted, and that a benign and mischievious ghost has manifested itself.

And there are accounts of flowers — violets — being placed on Lucy's grave for years, at least until 1983. No one knows how they came to be there.

Many of Pratt's detractors used the deaths of Carlisle students as proof that he was failing in his experiment to educate American Indians. One of these detractors was Spotted Tail himself, the chief from the Rosebud Agency, who had sent five children to Carlisle. In 1880 he made a trip there and registered many complaints. He did not want his sons in military uniforms. One of his sons was in the guardhouse. He wanted to pull all the Sioux children out, but Captain Pratt said the government was paying for their education and he could take his own children, but not the others. So, although his own children did not really wish to leave, Spotted Tail took them out anyway.

Was this school — this experiment — a failure?

Research gives us two sides. On one there are the stories of the runaways, the troublemakers. There is the fact that by 1910 over four thousand Indian children went through Carlisle, but fewer than six hundred were actual graduates. Many dropped out and returned home, only to find that they were regarded as aliens by their own people. And, because they had rejected their white schooling, they found themselves caught in a no-man's-land, between two worlds.

As part of the education offered at Carlisle, Captain Pratt helped many who wanted to return afterward to the reservation. He persuaded Indian agents to find them jobs as clerks in Indian agencies, on freighters, hauling goods for the Indians, or as herders for agency cattle.

Most of the graduates were able to earn a living away from the reservation. Others went on to higher education at Alma College in Michigan, Marietta College in Ohio, Rutgers University in New Jersey, or Millersville University or Dickinson College in Pennsylvania, and became doctors, teachers, artists, missionaries, and writers. Or renowned football players like Jim Thorpe.

The first class at Carlisle consisted of a little over a hundred boys and girls. By 1900 there was a student body of 1,218 Indians from seventy-six tribes.

The school operated for only thirty-nine years. But it seemed to set a pattern, for by 1900 there were twenty-five off-reservation boarding schools for American Indians, and the government was supporting eighty-one on-reservation boarding schools.

Many of these schools did not run as smoothly as Carlisle. Research from *American Indian Children at School*, by Michael C. Coleman, uncovers many cruelties inflicted on Indian students. There are reports out of the Phoenix

Indian School about runaway girls being made to cut the grass with scissors, and runaway boys being put in jail and made to wear dresses. One girl, who would not stop talking, had "an eraser shoved into her mouth. She sat there stiff with fright, head bent in shame and saliva dripping, until the teacher's sadistic appetite had been satisfied."

But there are the good things, too, such as a letter written by an Indian girl named Annie Thomas in 1891:

"I was born among the Pueblos and I went to Carlisle when I was a little girl. I had lived at the top of a hill, or pueblo, 500 feet high, so that I am an expert at climbing ladders. I am now climbing another kind of ladder. Sometimes it is very hard, but I still keep on climbing. I am now at the normal school at Fredonia, New York. I hope to reach the top someday and to be a schoolma'am."

Said Howard Whitewolf, Comanche: "The Indian young men and women who fail to get an education are like the warriors of the old days with their bows and arrows. The arrows would not reach [as] far as the white man's bullets. In the battles ahead, white men are trained to do business. If the Indian does not take this training, like a soldier drilling with his rifle, he will be cheated and lose money and land."

The first girls came to the Carlisle Indian School in 1879. Shown here are Sioux girls upon their arrival, wearing their traditional blanket clothing. Soon after, their clothes were taken from them, and they were forced to wear Victorian dresses, which was part of the school's effort to assimilate them.

Pictured here are Sioux children from the Pine Ridge Agency in 1887. School policy also required girls and boys to have their long hair cut off. This mandate was just one of many that conflicted with Indian customs, since Indians traditionally cut their hair to express grief.

184

This photograph features Annie Laurie, a Sioux girl, posed in full Indian dress.

Sioux Indians lived in tipis on the vast western plains of the United States. The drawings on the buffalo hides of the Sioux tipi in the foreground depict the Battle of the Little Bighorn (also known as Custer's Last Stand) when warriors from the Oglala Sioux, Hunkpapa Sioux, and Cheyenne tribes killed General George Armstrong Custer and his 225 soldiers while attempting to defend their winter hunting grounds in the Black Hills.

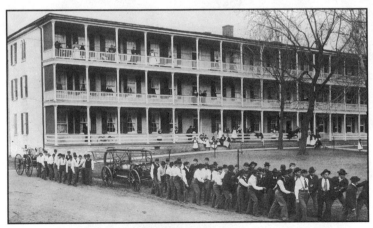

This fire drill in front of the girls' dormitory shows boys hauling portable water hoses. Boys were forced to give up their buffalo robes and to wear uniforms consisting of tailored pants, shirts, ties, and hats.

To encourage conversation in English, the school usually put three girls from different tribes in the same room. The room they shared was 14 feet by 16 feet in size. Furniture was provided by the school but the girls were allowed to decorate the room themselves. Rooms were inspected regularly and had to be kept tidy.

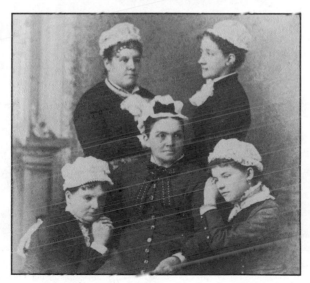

Pictured here are Carlisle Indian School teachers in 1880.

This classroom is occupied by ninth-grade students. The flexible curriculum allowed children to work at their own pace. Lessons included History, English, Physics, Chemistry, Geography, Mathematics, and Biology.

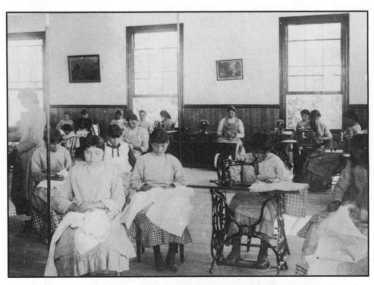

In addition to academic subjects, the curriculum for girls included sewing class, where they learned to make their own dresses. Practical skills such as sewing allowed the students to make useful items rather than buy them, and saved the school money.

Before children learned to speak English, they expressed memories of reservation life through pictographs similar to those that decorated tipi skins. This drawing by a young Sioux boy named Edgar Fire Thunder depicts an Indian courting ceremony. The Indian man, wrapped in his blanket, approaches the woman he hopes to make his wife, while his horse waits nearby.

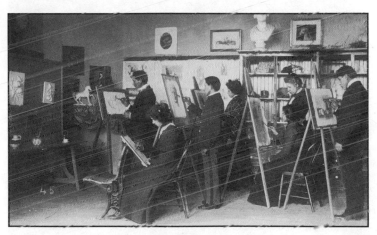

Students received formal art training at the Carlisle Indian School. In the school's continuing effort to acculturate them, students were encouraged to abandon pictograph drawing and to master the idealized scenes that were popular in American art at the time.

Workshops located on school grounds turned the students into an effective workforce. Children labored in carpentry, tailoring, shoemaking, and blacksmithing. Half the school day was devoted to work and the other half to studies. Extracurricular activities were scheduled for the evenings and weekends.

As a reward for hard work, students were permitted to attend Camp Sells, in the mountains near Pine Grove Park. They slept in tents, picked berries, and went fishing.

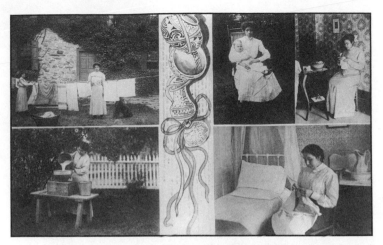

This postcard depicts scenes from a typical student outing. Exemplary students received permission to leave the school during the summer and to work for pay in the homes of local families. The money they earned was deposited in a school bank account and given to students on graduation. Pratt considered this project the supreme Americanizer.

CARLISLE INDIAN SCHOOL.

CARLISLE, PENNSYLVANIA _Nov._ 8 _190_ 0

M. FRIEDMAN, Supt.

Sir:

I want to go out into the country.

If you will send me I promise to OBEY MY EMPLOYER, TO KEEP ALL THE RULES OF THE SCHOOL.

I will attend Sunday School and Church regularly.

I will not absent myself from my farm home without permission of my employer and will not loaf about stores or elsewhere evenings or Sundays.

I will not make a practice of staying for meals when I visit my friends.

I will not use tobacco nor any spirituous liquors in any form.

I will not play cards nor gamble, and will save as much money as possible.

If out for the winter I will attend school regularly and will do my best to advance myself in my studies.

I will bathe regularly, write my home letter every month, and do all that I can to please my employer, improve myself and make the best use of the chance given me.   Very respectfully,

Alice M Bellanger, Pupil.

NOTE—This request is to be signed in triplicate, one copy to be kept by pupil, one retained in Superintendent's office, and one sent to employer.

Students submitted written requests for permission to go on an outing. This request from a student details the strict rules she will follow when off school grounds.

General Richard Henry Pratt founded the Carlisle Indian School because he believed that Indians could become productive members of society if given opportunities equal to those available to citizens. Although his intentions may have been good, many of the means taken at the school were extreme. Under these rigorous conditions, some children thrived and some did not.

Sioux Chief Spotted Tail (left) initially opposed sending children to the Carlisle Indian School because he did not want them taught by white men. The Sioux Indians had reason not to trust the white man: Three years following the discovery of gold in the Black Hills of Dakota in 1874, the U.S. government confiscated the land, violating the Fort Laramie Treaty of 1868, which recognized that territory as part of the Great Sioux Reservation. In the end, Spotted Tail did not think Pratt's experiment was beneficial to Indian children.

SCHOOL SONG

Nestling 'neath the mountains blue,

    Old Carlisle, our fair Carlisle.

We n'er can pay our debt to you,

    Old Carlisle, our fair Carlisle.

While the years roll swiftly by,

In our thoughts thou'rt always nigh,

To honor thee we'll ever try,

    Old Carlisle, our dear Carlisle.

All your precepts we hold dear,

    Old Carlisle, our fair Carlisle.

The world we'll face without a fear,

    Old Carlisle, our fair Carlisle.

Rememb'ring thee, we'll never fail,

We'll weather every storm and gale,

While o'er life's troubled sea we sail,

    Old Carlisle, our dear Carlisle.

The Carlisle Indian School song's patriotic lyrics may have been an attempt to boost morale and school spirit.

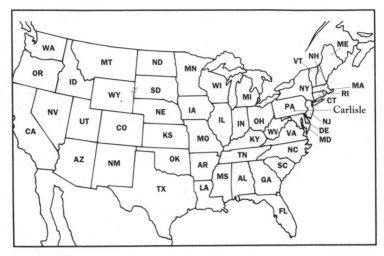

This modern map of the United States shows the approximate location of Carlisle, Pennsylvania, where the school was located.

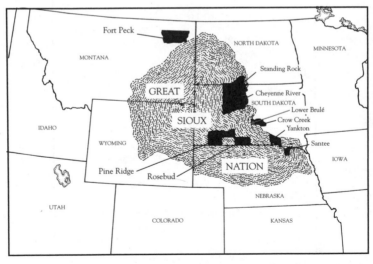

This detail shows the land that was the Great Sioux Nation in the mid 1800s. Areas in black indicate what are today the Sioux reservations.

About the Author

ANN RINALDI says about writing this book, "In doing historical research I ran across the story of the Indian School in Carlisle, Pennsylvania, and the heart-wrenching accounts of young Native Americans shipped across the country, away from their tribal culture, families, and familiar surroundings, to live in a hostile and strange environment. These children were made to learn the language and give up all the accoutrements of their own lifestyles. Here was a story that must be told, I decided. So I went to Carlisle, site of Captain Richard Henry Pratt's 'noble experiment,' to see for myself.

"There I found the Indian burial ground, with dozens of white headstones bearing the names of the Native American children from all tribes who had died while at the school. The names, with the tribes inscribed underneath, were so lyrical that they leapt out at me and took on instant personalities. Although many of these children attended Carlisle at dates later than that of my story, I used some of their names for classmates of Nannie Little Rose.

In one respect I hoped to bring them alive again and show their plight and their accomplishments to young readers today.

"Many of the events in the book, such as the journey across the country by Wapka, the Potawatomi boy who starved and worked his way to Carlisle; the fire that broke out in the school; and the instance of the little white daughter of one of the teachers who wanted a playhouse and got one made out of an outhouse, are based on reports in *Eadle keatah toh*, or *The Morning Star*, the school newspaper. Some Indian names were taken from this newspaper, also. Although some of these incidents happened at later dates, I feel they best depict the tone and mood of the school.

"Like Lucy Pretty Eagle, not all the children in the book were at Carlisle that first year. But like Lucy Pretty Eagle, their personalities came through to me with such force and inspiration, I had to use them. I am sure that in whatever Happy Hunting Ground they now reside, they will forgive this artistic license, and even smile upon it."

Ann Rinaldi is the well-known author of eighteen distinguished historical novels. She travels widely to research each of her books and is highly regarded for her impeccable and sensitive research. Her books have been named

ALA Best Books for Young Adults, CBC/IRA Young Adult Choices, and New York Public Library Books for the Teen Age. *Mine Eyes Have Seen* and *Second Bend in the River*, an *American Bookseller* "Pick of the Lists," are her most recent titles for Scholastic Press. She lives in Somerville, New Jersey, with her husband.

*In memory of my
uncle Anthony*

Acknowledgments

I would like to thank the librarians and staff of the Archives Branch of the U.S. Army Military History Institute at Carlisle Barracks, Carlisle, Pennsylvania, for their help and cooperation, as well as the authors of the many factual historical works I used to study the Carlisle Indian School and the Lakota Sioux Indians. Particularly valuable sources were *Sister to the Sioux: The Memoirs of Elaine Goodale Eastman; Waterlily* by Ella Cara Deloria; and *Lakota Belief and Ritual* by James R. Walker. Thank you, also, to Genevieve Bell, Ph.D., Department of Anthropology, Stanford University, for fact-checking the manuscript, and to my editor at Scholastic, Tracy Mack, for her support and understanding.

Grateful acknowledgment is made for permission to reprint the following:

Cover portrait: *Indian Girl, Little Star*. Painting by James Bama © 1973

Cover background: Student March, 1892. Photograph by John N. Choate. Courtesy of the Cumberland County Historical Society, Carlisle, Pennsylvania

Page 184 (top): Indian girls, Cumberland County Historical Society, Carlisle, Pennsylvania
   (bottom): Sioux children from Pine Ridge Agency, ibid.
Page 185: Annie Laurie, a Sioux girl, ibid.
Page 186 (top): Sioux tipi, photograph by Frank B. Fiske, courtesy Azusa Publishing, Inc., Englewood, Colorado
   (bottom): Fire drill, Cumberland County Historical Society, Carlisle, Pennsylvania
Page 187 (top): Interior of girls' dormitory, ibid.
   (bottom): Carlisle Indian School teachers, ibid.
Page 188 (top): Interior of school classroom, ibid.
   (bottom): Sewing classroom, ibid.
Page 189 (top): Indian pictograph, ibid.
   (bottom): Art classroom, ibid.
Page 190 (top): Carlisle Indian School Workshops, ibid.
   (bottom): Camp Sells, ibid.

Page 191 (top): Outing postcard, ibid.

         (bottom): Written request, ibid.

Page 192 (top): Richard Henry Pratt, ibid.

         (bottom): Spotted Tail, ibid.

Page 193: School song, ibid.

Page 194: Maps by Heather Saunders

Other books in the Dear America series

A Journey to the New World
The Diary of Remember Patience Whipple
by Kathryn Lasky

The Winter of Red Snow
The Revolutionary War Diary of Abigail Jane Stewart
by Kristiana Gregory

When Will This Cruel War Be Over?
The Civil War Diary of Emma Simpson
by Barry Denenberg

A Picture of Freedom
The Diary of Clotee, a Slave Girl
by Patricia C. McKissack

Across the Wide and Lonesome Prairie
The Oregon Trail Diary of Hattie Campbell
by Kristiana Gregory

So Far from Home
The Diary of Mary Driscoll, an Irish Mill Girl
by Barry Denenberg

I Thought My Soul Would Rise and Fly
The Diary of Patsy, a Freed Girl
by Joyce Hansen

West to a Land of Plenty
The Diary of Teresa Angelino Viscardi
by Jim Murphy

Dreams in the Golden Country
The Diary of Zipporah Feldman, a Jewish Immigrant Girl
by Kathryn Lasky

A Line in the Sand
The Alamo Diary of Lucinda Lawrence
by Sherry Garland

Standing in the Light
The Captive Diary of Catharine Carey Logan
by Mary Pope Osborne

Voyage on the Great Titanic
The Diary of Margaret Ann Brady
by Ellen Emerson White

The Great Railroad Race
The Diary of Libby West
by Kristiana Gregory

Copyright © 1999 by Ann Rinaldi

All rights reserved. Published by Scholastic Inc.
555 Broadway, New York, New York 10012.
DEAR AMERICA and the DEAR AMERICA logo are trademarks of
Scholastic Inc.

Library of Congress Cataloging-in-Publication Data
Rinaldi, Ann.
My heart is on the ground: the diary of Nannie Little Rose, a Sioux girl /
by Ann Rinaldi
p. cm. — (Dear America; 12)
Summary: In the diary account of her life at a government-run Pennsylvania
boarding school in 1880, a twelve-year-old Sioux Indian girl reveals a great
need to find a way to help her people.
ISBN 0-590-14922-6 (hardcover: alk. paper)
1. Dakota Indians — Juvenile fiction.
[1. Dakota Indians — Fiction.   2. Indians of North America.
3. Boarding schools — Fiction.   4. Schools — Fiction.]
I. Title.   II. Series.
PZ7.R459My 1999
[Fic] — dc21   LC #:98-26767
CIP AC
10 9 8 7 6 5 4 3 2 1   9/9 0/0 01 02 03

The display type was set in Sanvito.
The text type was set in Goudy.
Book design by Elizabeth B. Parisi

Printed in the U.S.A. 23
First edition, April 1999